1/13 Dres

Travis came around to Melissa's side of the Jeep

She lowered the window. Their faces were only inches apart. It was madness, but she ached for him to kiss her. If he ever got the urge, would he pretend she was his wife? She couldn't bear the thought.

His eyes played over her features. "You made this evening more memorable for us than you know," he said. She felt his warm breath on her mouth. Only a little closer… "How do I thank you?"

The blood pounded in her ears. "You're already doing that by agreeing to track down the people making our family's life miserable. It's a miracle you've already unearthed so much. Who else but a Texas Ranger could do what you've done?"

He let out a sigh. Maybe he didn't like remembering he had a job to do. "Speaking of your case, I was wondering if tomorrow you'd go hiking in the forest beyond the ridge with me. Since we're going to a new area, I thought we'd take my truck. Bring a backpack with the things you'll want."

What Melissa wanted was right here, and she didn't want to have to wait until tomorrow. "I'll be ready."

Dear Reader,

Have you ever been told you looked like someone else, or that someone else looked like you?

Did you like being compared?

Several times in life I've been told I looked like someone else, or acted like someone else, and I didn't like it. I wanted to be ME. It gets into all the questions of comparisons, whether good or bad. Though we simply brush off these comments and go on, I think we all care to varying degrees.

In *The Texas Ranger's Reward*, I thought about this problem and decided to magnify it to the point that it becomes one of the linchpins of the plot concerning the hero and heroine. Strongly resembling someone else can lead to all kinds of consequences. In my story it raises doubts, picks away at self confidence, arouses anger, destroys trust. The more I wrote, the more fascinated I became to see the way it produced so many issues on so many levels. I hope as you read, you'll find this element in my story fascinating, too. Most of all, I hope you'll find the resolution satisfying.

Enjoy!

Rebecca Winters

The Texas Ranger's Reward

REBECCA WINTERS

HARLEQUIN®

entertain, enrich, inspire™

Recycling programs
for this product may
not exist in your area.

ISBN-13: 978-0-373-75426-7

THE TEXAS RANGER'S REWARD

www.Harlequin.com

Printed in U.S.A.

ABOUT THE AUTHOR

Rebecca Winters, whose family of four children has now swelled to include five beautiful grandchildren, lives in Salt Lake City, Utah, in the land of the Rocky Mountains. With canyons and high alpine meadows full of wildflowers, she never runs out of places to explore. They, plus her favorite vacation spots in Europe, often end up as backgrounds for her romance novels, because writing is her passion, along with her family and church. Rebecca loves to hear from readers. If you wish to email her, please visit her website, www.cleanromances.com.

Books by Rebecca Winters
HARLEQUIN AMERICAN ROMANCE

To my dear sister Kathie, who is kind enough to read my novels and always gets the essence of what I'm trying to say. Even better, we have long discussions that thrill my heart.

Chapter One

Melissa Dalton pulled her red-and-black Jeep Wrangler into the parking lot outside the entrance to the Lone Peak Children's Physical Therapy Clinic with no time to spare before her first appointment at eight-thirty. She lived on Salt Lake City's southeast bench, in the Sandy area, close to the Wasatch Mountains, and the new facility was only five minutes from her town-house condo.

How typical of her that even though she lived so close, she was still going to be late!

Waving to her friend Rosie, another therapist who'd just arrived, she hurried into the building and then her office, ready to go. As was her custom, she'd caught her shoulder-length hair at her nape so it wouldn't get in the way while she worked with one of her patients.

Today she'd worn a floppy French clip bow in navy to match her short-sleeved navy-and-white print top, and designer jeans. She'd put pearl studs in her ears. Melissa believed in dressing up as much as possible so she wouldn't look clinical. No lab coat for her. It made the kids nervous. Children who had to see her on a regular basis liked it when she came wearing something fashionable.

What she wore on her feet had to be comfortable for work, of course, but little girls often commented on her cute candy-apple-red flats. And her bangle bracelets, which came in gold, silver and jeweled tones. It was also important that she smelled good and kept her nails manicured. Children noticed everything. When she was looking her best, the sessions seemed brighter for the kids. Which made Melissa feel better about herself.

After the trauma leading up to her divorce six years ago, she'd gone through a period where she hadn't paid attention to her clothes or hair. But once she'd gone into pediatric orthopedic physical therapy, the children asked so many personal questions that she'd begun to look at herself again and care about her appearance. It was her young patients who helped pull her out of her depression. She loved them and enjoyed working with them.

Susan, the receptionist, had put a new file on her desk. It was a pertinent history sent by a doctor. Melissa sat down in her swivel chair to read it.

Casey Stillman, Salt Lake, seven, broken left femur after fall from a horse July 27. Plated and screwed while in surgery. See X-rays. Successful. Anticipate complete recovery. Given crutches. Was home-schooled during recuperation period. As of Friday, September 7, father indicates son still clings to crutches and is anxious about bearing weight. Patient should be done with them. No physical reason for them now. Is afraid to go to school. Recommend therapy. Pain and muscle soreness expressed, but wonder if there's a psychological issue.

Melissa glanced at the calendar. It was September 10. At more than five weeks following an accident, most children were pretty well back to normal, but others…

"Take as long as you need, bud. It's okay." Concerned by his lack of progress, Travis Stillman eyed his son, who was still dependant on his crutches. According to the doctor, Casey shouldn't need them anymore, thus the referral to visit someone who could work with him.

Halfway from Travis's blue Altima to the door of the clinic, Casey stopped. "My leg hurts." He was close to tears.

"I know, but pretty soon it will go away." Travis prayed that was true. Today was Monday, Casey's twentieth day of missing school. Though he'd kept up with his lessons at home, who knew how long it would take before he was ready to rejoin his second-grade class?

Travis held the door as his son hobbled into the clinic. "I don't want to go in there," Casey wailed as they approached the front desk.

The receptionist smiled. "It won't take long." She indicated the therapist's office—the first door down the hall on the right.

Travis didn't dare offer to pick up his son and carry him. His boy was proud as blazes. Lately, Travis's sister, Pat, had been reminding him that Casey was a chip off the old block. But since his fall, too much pride had turned Casey into a hermit.

He wouldn't give up the crutches, and he didn't want to play with his cousins, let alone the neighbors' children. Forget going to school. Travis's friend Mitch Garrett, one of the P.I.s who worked with him at the Lufka Private Investigator firm in Salt Lake, had brought over his newly adopted son, Zack, several times to play. But Casey was having none of it—he'd been too down since the accident.

They were almost to the office in question when someone called out, "Hi, Casey! Wow! Look at you handle those crutches!"

The cheerful-sounding female voice caused Travis to look up. He did a triple take when he saw a knockout woman with ash-brown hair standing outside the office door. She looked like a model.

She walked toward them and stopped in front of Casey, making Travis aware of her flowery fragrance. "My name's Melissa. *You* look fine, but I want to hear what happened to your horse. Did it live?"

The question was so unexpected, Casey laughed. "Yes."

"What's his name?"

"Sugar."

"Isn't that kind of a wuss name?"

"Yes."

"Who's this with you?" Her dancing eyes lifted to Travis. For some reason the mix of blue and gray was disturbing to him, but he couldn't figure out why.

"My dad."

"How do you do, Dad," she teased. "Come with me, Casey, and let's talk about how boring it's been for you this past month."

A bemused Travis followed them and received another surprise when instead of into her office, she took them to the next door down the hall. The room turned out to be a sunny space containing physical therapy equipment. *What? No discussion first?*

While Travis looked on, the therapist said to Casey, "I'll take your crutches."

"What if I fall down?"

"I'll catch you."

Travis watched as his son thought about it, then gave them up. The therapist promptly put them on the floor. "Okay. Let's see you walk."

"I—I can't. My leg hurts."

"Don't you know that's a good thing?"

He blinked. "It is?"

"Absolutely. The muscles want to move and it means you're getting well. But if you'll walk without the crutches, it will help you get better even faster. Don't worry if it hurts. A little pain doesn't matter. My first dog lost his hind leg when a car hit him. He had to learn to walk on three legs, without any crutches."

"He did?"

"Yes, and it hurt to have to do that. But he was a trooper, and pretty soon all the pain went away. Have you ever had a dog?"

"Yes. We've got one now. He's a Scottish terrier."

"What's his name?"

"Dexter."

"Well, then…you need to take Dexter on lots of walks, but you can't do that with those crutches. Let's walk around the room together. If you think you're going to fall, put out your hand."

"Okay."

Travis was astonished that his son would actually do as she asked. When he began taking one tentative step, then another, Travis was elated, but also experienced a feeling of resentment that this Melissa could get his son to perform so easily. The feeling grew when Casey reached for her only once in the journey around the big room. Casey was still favoring his left leg, but this was the most he'd walked without help since the operation!

Melissa picked up the crutches and fitted them back under his arms. "You walked perfectly. And even though it hurt, you're still alive, right?"

Casey nodded with a smile, a reaction that shocked Travis.

"Come to my office and I'll give you a prize for doing a brilliant job this morning."

"What kind of prize?"

The way Casey was chatting with the woman, you'd have thought they were old friends. The change in Casey's behavior was nothing short of amazing. Too amazing, Travis thought, before realizing he was being uncharitable. She'd been working wonders with his boy.

When they walked through the door, he thought they'd entered a children's art museum. On one of the walls a large corkboard was covered in childlike drawings pinned up with colored tacks. Two other walls contained framed, stylized superheroes and animals painted in bright colors. He didn't recognize any of them, which meant they were original—and totally riveting. Casey looked around in delight.

Along the wall by the door sat a big pirate treasure chest. When the therapist opened the lid, Travis saw it was chock-full of store-bought toys in their packaging. This was much better than getting a look inside Santa's pack. Despite his conflicted feelings about Melissa, Travis couldn't seem to take his eyes off her sensational figure as she started rummaging through the toys.

"Hmm, let me see…" Travis could tell Casey's interest was piqued. In fact, he was getting impatient waiting for her to decide. "Ah. Here's the one I was looking for." She pulled out a package. "Hand me your crutches and I'll let you open it."

This time Casey hardly hesitated before he did her bidding. Travis could see that his son stood just fine without any support. She exchanged the crutches for the package. It took a minute for him to get it unwrapped.

"Look, Dad—a new leash for Dexter!" That was the biggest burst of happiness he'd heard from his son since before his fall. For the moment Casey had forgotten the pain in his leg.

"How about that, bud." Travis had tried bribery on him, but without the same result. Those were some pricey items he could see in that pirate chest. The therapist seemed to be doing everything right. His perturbance made no sense at all.

"When you get home, you'll have to take Dexter for a walk with it." She picked up the empty carton and tossed it in the wastebasket. "Want to give it to your dad to hold?"

Travis took it from him. The retractable leash would handle their twenty-two-pound Scottie without a problem.

After she'd helped him with his crutches, she said, "You can go home now."

Casey's eyes rounded. "You mean I don't have to get up on a table or anything?"

Her mouth curved into a big smile. "Nope. That's because you're all better. When you come back tomorrow morning, I'll let you look through the chest and pick out your own prize—*if* you walk all the way in from the car without your crutches. I'll be watching from the front door."

"I…think I'll be able to do it." His son was pretty transparent.

"Great! In that case I can't wait until tomorrow."

Casey grinned. "Thanks for the leash. Blue's my favorite color."

"Mine, too." She flicked her floppy bow to show him. Travis noted her bracelets, and saw she wore no rings on either hand. "I like blueberry popsicles, as well."

"So do I!" Casey actually laughed. "Are you really a doctor?"

"No, but don't I look like one?"

"No," Casey said. "You're too pretty."

Travis eyed his son in surprise.

"Well, thank you. I used to be a nurse. Then I trained

to become an orthopedic therapist. That means I work with patients after their doctor has seen them."

She finally glanced at Travis, just as he thought she'd forgotten him altogether. "We'll see you and your son in the morning. I'll put you down on my calendar for the same time, unless that's a problem."

"No. We'll be here at eight-thirty. Thank you."

"You're welcome. Bye, Casey."

"See ya," he called back.

Travis followed him out the door. Maybe it was his imagination, but he thought Casey walked most of the way, and used his crutches only for show. When they reached the car, Travis helped him in the back and fastened the seat belt.

In another minute they were on their way home. Instead of complaining, Casey played with the leash. "That was fun! I can't wait to get my prize tomorrow."

"Remember what Melissa said?"

"Yeah. I gotta walk all the way from the car into the building and not use my crutches. I can do that."

Travis smiled tightly and didn't ask any more questions. For the rest of the drive he remained immersed in thought. There'd been no preliminary discussion, and she'd given Travis no follow-up instructions. Nothing! It had irritated the hell out of him.

Not until he pulled in the driveway did he discover what was wrong with him.

There was an old saying about every person on earth having a double. This morning that saying had particular meaning for him.

He'd just come face-to-face with a woman who resembled, in looks and personality, his murdered wife, Valerie.

Travis was convinced that was the reason Casey had undergone a miraculous change at the therapist's hands. Although she was a younger version, Melissa Dalton had Valerie's sunny disposition and a way of making challenging things sound like fun. Her appealing energy had captured his son's attention, and he'd wanted her approval. But the very qualities about her that had caused the first therapy session to go so well haunted Travis.

He dreaded the thought of having to see her again in the morning. It had been fifteen months since he'd buried his wife in Texas. Melissa had unwittingly brought certain memories back to life. Casey's willingness to do what she wanted might have been unconscious, but his son had definitely responded because of deeply embedded memories, too.

It was going to be a long day and an even longer night, because Travis knew there'd be little sleep for him.

MELISSA LEFT FOR WORK on Tuesday morning curious to see if the skinny, brown-haired Stillman boy would let go of his crutches for good. She knew there was nothing wrong with him physically.

Probably never in her life had she seen such a handsome face or such sky-blue eyes. People would marvel over his remarkable features as he grew into manhood. Especially women. You needed to look no further than the boy's father.

But on the adult version—the man appeared to be

mid-thirties—there were differences. She'd seen the lines left by life and grief around his eyes and mouth, the shadow of a dark beard on his square jaw. The artist in her had caught the fierce gaze of arctic-blue eyes, distant and speculative. Almost forbidding. She shivered at the memory.

In the midst of her thoughts, she heard her cell ring. She reached for it and checked the caller ID. "Hi, Tom."

"Hey, how was your Labor Day weekend?"

"Semiproductive."

Unfortunately, she'd found herself looking over her shoulder quite a bit while doing her artwork. She'd been at the family cabin on her own, not for the first time this summer. Neither her parents, nor either of her two married siblings had used the place in August, yet increasingly she'd had a vague sense that someone other than herself had been there. Though she'd seen no signs of forced entry, there were little indications, such as books and lamps in places she didn't remember them being, the bedding not made up the normal way, and signs of dirty footprints on the floor by the back door. It made her nervous at night, so she'd turned on the generator, hoping the resulting sound and lights would ward off intruders.

If she'd still had her bulldog, Spike, Melissa wouldn't have felt so nervous. But soon after her divorce, her beloved pet had died of old age. She hadn't been able to bring herself to get a new one. She couldn't give an animal the time it deserved.

"Same here," Tom said, jolting her back to the present. "I'm afraid my children didn't leave me any time to write." That meant he'd had visitation through the long weekend. "I'm glad you're back. Let's meet for dinner at Rinaldo's in Bell Canyon Plaza after work."

"I'm afraid I can't. I promised the folks I'd spend the evening with them." Melissa needed to talk to her parents about the problem at the cabin. After their whole family had gotten together there for a Fourth of July celebration, her parents had gone to Laguna Beach, California, for two weeks on their own. "How about lunch there on Thursday?" She would have finished her renderings by then. "I'll bring everything you've been waiting for."

"Not till Thursday? I guess I can wait. What time?"

"One o'clock?" It would be right after the Denton baby's appointment. She had torticollis, a condition that curtailed her range of neck motion. Mrs. Denton fell apart emotionally every time she brought the baby for therapy. Melissa would need a break following the session.

"Okay, see you then. I'm looking forward to it."

Melissa hung up, unable to say the same thing back to him. Tom Hunt was a prominent patent attorney specializing in intellectual properties. He was also a talented writer of children's fiction. They'd met in March when he'd brought his son in for therapy because of knee pain. The eleven-year-old had Osgood-Schlatter disease, fortunately not too serious a case.

During the treatments, Tom had admired the paintings hanging in her office. When he'd learned she was the artist, he'd asked her if she'd be willing to do some sketches for a story he'd been working on. It was set during World War II, between two childhood friends whose countries were fighting on opposing sides. The subject appealed to her and she'd said yes. She'd started working closely with Tom, but despite his obvious interest, she had no desire for any sort of romantic relationship with him.

She knew he wanted to get married again, but in truth, the thought of marrying again herself filled her with dread.

Melissa had been young and in love when she'd married exciting, handsome Russell Dalton. But her dreams of living happily ever after were shattered when she realized she'd married an abuser.

Their seven-month marriage had come to an abrupt end the day he got home from his last college class. She was studying for finals at the kitchen table when he walked in, wanting to make love. Melissa had told him she needed to keep on studying, but he wouldn't take no for an answer. He'd jerked her out of the chair like a rag doll.

Shocked, she'd tried to push him away, and he'd responded by slapping her in the face so hard she fell to the floor. That blow had changed her life.

Though he was remorseful and swore it would never happen again, she'd grabbed her keys and run from the apartment and their life together. Divorce had followed.

Intellectually, she knew there were good men out in the universe who would make fine husbands. Over the past six years she'd dated quite a few of them. But the thought of taking the critical step into another marriage left her apprehensive.

To make her feelings clear to Tom, she never went out with him in the evening, or worked with him when his two children were on visitation. She shied away from any attachments. It wasn't fair to his kids, when there could be no future. He should have gotten the point long before now.

Since her divorce, Melissa had reached a restful place where she was in control. She wanted to stay there. When Tom's book was finished to his specifications, she'd decided, it would be the only project she'd do with him. After that, there wouldn't be a reason to get together again, and they could part with no hard feelings.

After parking in her usual spot, she headed for the clinic doors. She was almost there when she heard her name being called. Melissa turned to see Casey Stillman walking carefully away from a blue car toward her. He was dressed in shorts and a white T-shirt. His father followed, carrying the crutches.

She felt a burst of pleasure at the boy's taking up the challenge. When Casey was about halfway to her, he hesitated. "Keep coming, Casey!" she called. "You're doing great!"

The boy got a determined look on his face and picked up his speed. Once he reached her, she gave him a quick hug. "I'm very proud of you."

He looked up at her and smiled. Children smiled at her every day, but for some reason she didn't understand, Casey's expression tugged at her emotions. "It doesn't hurt that much."

"That's because you're so tough!" She let go of his

shoulders. "Come into my office. You've earned a gift of your choice. Do you need your crutches to get inside?"

Casey stared at her. "Will you hold my hand?"

"Of course." She took his hand and they walked through the main doors to her suite. She made sure they didn't go too fast. He was still favoring his leg, but not nearly as much as the day before.

Melissa walked him over to the treasure chest and opened it. "Take all the time you want picking out your prize. If you get tired, here's a little stool to sit on while you look."

He propped himself on the edge of the chest and started going through the presents. While he was occupied, she moved to her desk across the room and sat behind it. Casey's hard-muscled father, in jeans and a dark green sport shirt, took a chair opposite her and placed the crutches on the floor next to him.

"Mr. Stillman," she began quietly, "the doctor suggested your son's problem was psychological, so that's why I threw him in at the deep end of the pool yesterday. It's clear his leg has healed and he's able to walk just fine. Do you know any reason why his problem may have been so easily resolved? I don't. I know I'm close to being the perfect therapist, but an overnight recovery is astonishing."

The man's lips quirked at her joke, but she got the impression there was something about her he didn't like. She saw it in his wintry eyes. An odd chill went through her.

"I've discovered there's a very good reason," he answered, in a low voice so deep it resonated through her body. "But I would prefer to tell you out of his hearing." Casey's dad looked at her with such solemnity she took a quick breath.

"Understood. Since I'd like one more session with him, tomorrow morning, could you call me this afternoon? Say, around one? That's when I take my lunch break, and we can talk."

"I'll see that Casey is otherwise occupied, then phone you."

"Melissa?" his son called. "Can I have this Captain America toy?"

"Sure. It's one of my favorites. The gizmo shoots little disks."

"Awesome!"

"Did you know there's something else I'd like you to do for me?"

"What?"

"Just use one crutch on your way out to your father's car. Think you can do that?"

"Yes," he said. But he was so absorbed with his new toy she doubted he'd really listened. In a few long strides, his dad, carrying both crutches, reached Casey. He fitted one under his son's arm, then took the gift from him.

Melissa stood up. "I have one more favor to ask you, Casey." He finally lifted his head. "Will you come to my office tomorrow without your crutches? Just leave them at home. If you do that, I've got another surprise for you."

"Is it in the pirate chest?"

"I had something else in mind, but if there's another toy you'd like in there, that's fine."

She could almost hear his brain working. "Will I like it a lot?"

Kids. She loved them.

"I can guarantee it."

His eyes lit up. "Okay."

"Then I'll see you tomorrow. Bye, Casey."

"Can you thank her for being so generous?" his father prodded.

"Thanks, Melissa."

"You're welcome." She closed the door behind them to get ready for her next patient.

The morning seemed to pass much slower than usual. Melissa knew why. She was waiting for lunch, when Casey's father was supposed to phone. Not once in three years had she been given a case where it was over almost before it had begun. Mr. Stillman had indicated he knew the reason for his son's capitulation. She was eager for him to share it with her.

After her last appointment, she took a bottle of juice from her mini fridge and drank it while she typed the last patient's follow-up notes into the computer. At five after one, the receptionist told her she was wanted on line three. She picked up the receiver.

"Melissa Dalton speaking."

"This is Travis Stillman."

"Thanks for calling me, Mr. Stillman. Where is Casey right now?"

"In the kitchen eating lunch with the housekeeper. He's using her and Dexter to retrieve those disks."

She laughed softly. "From what I saw this morning, he should be picking them up himself. In my professional opinion he has healed beautifully. So why did he cling to the crutches until you brought him to the clinic?"

"Let me give you a bit of background first. Until fifteen months ago, I was a Texas Ranger living with my wife and son in Fort Davis, Texas."

A Texas Ranger. In Melissa's mind, Texas Rangers were legendary, and he fitted her image of one exactly.

"On my last case," he went on, "I went after a gang in a brutal racial slaying. I caught up with two of them, but a third one eluded me. They were known as the McClusky brothers. Soon after their capture, the third brother, Danny McClusky, murdered my wife in cold blood while she was driving home from the grocery store. It was a revenge killing. Thankfully, Casey was still at school."

His revelation stopped her cold. "I—I can't imagine anything so horrifying," she stammered. "Is that killer still free?"

"Yes. He's on the FBI's most wanted list. They'll get him in time."

"How do you live with that?"

"Not so well. Two other times during my career, my wife and son were threatened. After I buried her, I decided enough was enough, and resigned from the Texas Rangers. Casey needs me too much."

"He's so lucky you're still alive!" she said, before she realized how emotional she sounded. She knew what it felt like to be threatened. She'd gotten out of her marriage because of it. For both his and Casey's sakes, she was glad Mr. Stillman had moved to Utah, away from danger.

"I have a sister," he said, "who lives in Lone Peak Estates here in Sandy, with her husband and their two kids. Since the area's zoned for horses, she encouraged us to move across the street from her so we could ride their horses when we wanted. After the loss of his mother, I wanted Casey to have family close by."

"Of course," Melissa murmured, still shocked by the tragic story. For a child to lose his mother like that was utterly heartbreaking.

"He's had a hard time," Mr. Stillman continued, "but we were doing better until he fell off his horse and broke his leg. It happened soon after Pioneer Day, on the twenty-fourth of July. Having the surgery frightened him and set him back emotionally. He's been crying for his mother at night."

"That's only natural. Who wouldn't? In hellish times the child in everyone cries for his or her mother."

Melissa had wanted to cry in her mom's arms in the months before she'd run from Russ, wanting her to make everything all right. But she'd felt too ashamed to tell her parents anything. They'd advised her to wait another year before she got married, just to be sure. But oh, no. She knew what she was doing. What a fool.

She hadn't confided in her parents until after she'd left Russ.

Poor Casey hadn't had his mother when he'd fallen.

"When you greeted him outside your office yesterday morning, it was like something magical happened—he responded to you without even thinking about it. I was bewildered by his reaction until we got home. That's when I realized there's something about you that reminds him of his mother—the way you talk, your enthusiasm, even your physical appearance. You have a vitality like hers. Put all that together and you could be her double."

"Really?"

"Yes. At this point I believe he'd do anything for you. He proved that today."

Mr. Stillman had just given her a plausible answer for Casey's quick turnaround, but his own reaction was far more complicated. Melissa jumped up from her chair, suddenly putting two and two together. Whether he'd had a good, mediocre or bad marriage, seeing someone who reminded him so strongly of his wife must have come as a shock to him.

She'd known something was wrong. For some reason it made her feel strange. She didn't want to look like anyone else, especially his murdered wife. Apparently he didn't like it, either.

"Thank you for telling me all this," she said. "Considering his progress, tomorrow should be the last time he needs to come in." Working with children had made her careful not to allow attachments to form. "I'll send you home with a sheet showing a few exercises he can do. If you make a game of it and do them with him, he won't know you're trying to help strengthen those muscles. Keep in mind he doesn't have to do the exercises. Natural play will eventually work out any kinks, but it's something you can do together as father and son to speed things up. Do you have any questions for me?"

"None."

He seemed anxious to get off the phone. "Then I'll see you in the morning. We'll deal with the issue of his not wanting to go to school then."

Melissa hung up. She had no desire to prolong their conversation either. It would have been agony for Travis Stillman to have to discuss the tragedy with her. Heaven knows it was hard enough to hear about it. Any trauma that directly affected a child pained her. But murder… The poor boy. The poor father. He'd been forced to give up his life's work and move to a new state. None of that could have been easy.

She was glad she had a busy schedule that afternoon. It would get her mind off what she'd learned.

At four o'clock she left the clinic for her parents' home in Federal Heights, an area in the northeast region of the city near the University of Utah. Five generations of Robertses, all of whom had run the Wasatch Front Steel Corporation, had lived there. Melissa had grown up surrounded by tall, gorgeous old trees and a lush yard. Her town house, where the trees had been newly planted and there was no heavy foliage, was a big change.

While she ate dinner with her parents, she told them about the cabin. Her father rubbed his chin. "That's the trouble with such remote places, honey. After every winter, our neighbors up there complain of the same thing. Somebody's broken in and things are stolen."

She shook her head "Winter is one thing, Dad, but

for intruders to be that brazen in summer is really up-
setting. I didn't see anything missing, but I know someone has been in there since July 24."

"Let's just be thankful you didn't surprise them when
you walked in," her mother said. "I've never liked you
going up there alone. This settles it. Please don't use the
cabin again unless you have a friend or family mem-
ber with you."

"Mom—"

"I don't care if you're a grown woman, Melissa. It's
not safe."

"Your mother's right, honey. What about Tom?"

"He's a man I've done some artwork for, but that's
all. I've never been interested in him. When the book's
done, I won't be doing any more projects with him.
Real-life paintings aren't the kind of thing I like to do."

Her dad glanced at her with affection. "I know. You
love your world of fantasy."

"I always have." She put down her fork. "Fall is when
I like to be up at the cabin every weekend. The at-
mosphere inspires me. My week's vacation starts next
Tuesday. I planned to live up there the whole time, so
I can hike and paint nonstop."

"If you're determined to go alone," her father said,
"then you need to buy a gun and learn how to shoot it."

Her mother gasped. "William!"

"Well, it's either that or take a boyfriend along." Her
parents despaired of her ever settling down again, and
brought up the subject at every opportunity.

"I don't have one. What if we hired a retired police-
man to be at the cabin when I go up? I'd help pay him."

Her father eyed her in frustration. "I guess anything's possible, but tell you what, honey. Some time tomorrow I'll call the police in the Kamas area and ask them to send someone over to the cabin and take a look."

"I don't see any signs of a break-in, so I don't think that will do any good."

"You have a point. Let me think about it. I don't like this any more than you do."

Her mother leaned forward. "I'll go up with you for a couple of nights, and I'm sure John and Linda will, too. In the meantime, why don't you ask Rosie from your work?"

"She's involved with a guy, Mom."

Besides, the problem with taking girl friends up there was that they needed to be entertained. At night they wanted to drive down to Kamas for a little fun, and to meet the local male talent. Melissa had done that years ago. It was how she'd met her husband. She had no desire for lightning to strike her twice in the same place.

Chapter Two

Travis was awake Wednesday morning long before it was time to take Casey to the clinic. His boss, Roman Lufka, owner of the Lufka Private Investigator firm, had intended to assign him a new case on Monday, but because Travis's son refused to go to school, the timing was wrong.

Roman was the greatest, and told him to take as long as he needed to work with Casey, but Travis was getting anxious. It was one thing for his son to convince the therapist that he could manage without his crutches in order to receive a prize, and quite another to agree to go back to school without them.

Travis heard his cell phone ringing when he came out of the shower. Hitching a towel around his hips, he hurried into the bedroom and reached for it. Maybe the therapist was calling because a scheduling problem had come up.

Last night, without knowing what he knew, his housekeeper, Deana White, had whispered to him that Casey seemed to have developed a crush on the therapist and couldn't wait until morning. Travis didn't want to think about the damage a cancelation could do at such a pivotal point in Casey's recovery.

Relief swept through him when he looked at the caller ID before picking up. "Hey, Chaz, it's good to hear your voice." Chaz Roylance was another great friend he'd made at the firm.

"Do you and Casey want to meet up for breakfast? I'll bring Abby." All the guys were trying to help Travis get through this rough period with his son.

"There's nothing I'd like better, but we're due at his therapist's in twenty minutes."

"How's it going?"

Travis sucked in his breath. "She challenged him to come without his crutches. Wants him to leave them at home. If he takes her up on it, I think we're halfway there."

"Only halfway?"

"The other half is getting him to go back to school."

"I hear you. As you know, our Abby is still having meltdowns over bees."

"The poor little tyke."

"When she sees one, it's the end of the world. Frankly, I'm glad cooler weather is on the way. Unless I can promise that bees won't be around, she refuses to do certain things, even for her mother."

For her mother.

In that arena, Travis had the edge on Chaz, because the therapist seemed to have the power to get his son to do anything. Travis ought to be grateful to her. Hell, he *was* grateful, but nothing seemed to alleviate his tortured thoughts since he'd met her.

"Thanks for the invite," he said to Chaz. "I'll call you tomorrow." He hung up and went back to the bathroom to shave. After putting on a crew-neck and dark trousers, he walked through the house to find his son in the kitchen eating breakfast. He'd dressed in jeans and a T-shirt. Travis didn't know if Deana had helped him or not.

And so far Casey hadn't gotten bored with Captain America.

"Good morning." The housekeeper, who'd raised three children of her own, put a plate of sausages and pancakes in front of him.

"Thanks, Deana."

Travis didn't have much appetite, but he ate what she'd served him, to be polite. His sister, Pat, had helped him find Deana. She'd been coming once a week to clean, and the rest of the time she picked up Casey from school and got dinner ready. Since he'd broken his leg, however, Deana had been putting in long hours, and Casey liked her.

Lately he hadn't been interested in food, and today he'd left half his breakfast on his plate, Travis noted in concern. "Hey, bud, it's time to go to the clinic. Put the toy down, okay?"

"Okay. What do you think she's going to give me this morning?"

He studied his son. "Are you going to leave your crutches here?"

Casey had laid them on the floor by his chair. "Yup."

"Then let's get going and find out. Do you need me to hold your hand?"

"I don't think so."

Deana sent Travis a private smile. What she didn't know was that although this was progress, the difficult part—school—was still to come. But he'd wait until they were in the therapist's office to bring the subject up.

Dexter followed them to the garage, and Casey gave him a hug. If people didn't look too closely, they might never know Casey had gone through his ordeal, Travis decided. Though his son took a little more time, he walked with a steady gait. Like any child, he loved getting neat things, but Travis feared that another gift wasn't all that was motivating him.

"There she is!" Casey spotted Melissa as they drove into the clinic parking lot five minutes later. There weren't many cars this early. When Casey climbed out she started waving. This time Travis didn't see any hesitancy on his son's part as he closed the distance between them.

Travis brought up the rear, surreptitiously studying Melissa Dalton. This morning she was turned out in a pair of latte-colored trousers with a dark brown waistband. With the fitted melon-colored blouse, it was hard to look anywhere else.

Her eyes appraised Casey. "Well, look at you. Good as new!" The boy beamed up at her. "I like a guy who makes a promise and keeps it. Where are those old crutches?"

"At home. I turned them into weapons." Travis blinked when Casey unexpectedly pulled a folded paper from his pocket and handed it to her. "See?"

"Hmm. What have we got here?" He giggled while she opened the paper with great ceremony. "Whoa, I certainly *do* see. How clever of you to make them into laser guns! Is that an interplanetary rocket they fit on?"

"Yeah."

She pressed it to her heart. "Can I have this and put it up on the corkboard for the other children to see?"

He nodded.

"When we get inside, you have to autograph it."

"Auto—?"

"*Autograph's* a fancy word for your name."

"Okay. I can print it."

"I didn't doubt it for a second. Come with me."

Once the three of them reached her office, Melissa walked around the desk and opened the top drawer. "Here's a good pen, Casey. Take the drawing over to the table by the books. After you print your name, you can put up your picture using those tacks on the board."

"Where shall I print it?"

"Anyplace you like. Make sure it's big so everyone can see it."

Casey got down on his knees to get to work. That's when Travis knew his son was no longer thinking about his leg. He chuckled as Casey's tongue rubbed against his lower lip while he carried out her suggestion.

"Here," she said when he was done, "I'll make a little more room for it." While she helped Casey mount the drawing, Travis returned the felt-tipped pen to her desk, then wandered over to see the finished product. But he found himself looking at the skein of lustrous hair caught at the nape of her neck with a coral flower clip. This morning she wore gold studs in her earlobes. Her fashion sense held strong appeal for him. Almost as much as her gorgeous body did.

"I love it!" she declared, drawing Travis's attention back to the drawing. His son had put his name coming out of the tip of the rocket, with each letter getting a little bigger. "I especially like the way you make your *y* with the curlicue on the tail."

Casey smiled again. Every time she opened her mouth, she built his son's confidence, Travis realized.

"This calls for a celebration." She walked back to her desk and reached in the drawer for a small envelope. Handing it to Casey, she said, "Inside this are three passes for your dad to take you and a close friend to a fun movie. And I have one more thing for you. It's in the clinic kitchen. I'll be right back."

Travis felt the gift giving had gone on long enough, and would have told her so, but she left the office too fast. He sat down with Casey. "That was certainly nice of her. Be sure to thank her for those passes when she comes back in."

"I will," he answered, sounding preoccupied. Travis didn't know how Casey felt about his latest present, but was glad he didn't say he'd have preferred a toy. "Hey, Dad, look at the picture of the huge bulldog! I wish I could take that one home."

Travis automatically complied, glancing toward the fabulous collection as he shook his head.

"Sorry, bud. That one stays on the wall." If he had a dollar for every time his son wished for something...

Pretty soon Melissa came back with a bakery carton

of iced cupcakes decorated in autumn colors, and put it on the table with some napkins.

"I noticed on your medical chart that you had a birthday a couple of weeks ago," she said, "but since you weren't in school, you didn't have a chance to celebrate. Every kid celebrates birthdays at school. Today would be the perfect day to take these to class. The other kids will love a treat. There's enough in the box for the three of us to have one before your dad drives you to school. Your teacher's waiting for you."

Casey looked as dumbfounded as Travis felt. "She is?"

"Of course. Doesn't everyone go to school on Wednesdays?" Casey nodded. "She's looking for one Mr. Casey Stillman to show up. Did you meet her at a parent-teacher conference before school started?"

"No. I couldn't walk."

"Well, you can now! Here—try one." She opened the lid. "You pick the color you want."

At first Casey couldn't decide. Travis reached for a yellow one and ate it in two bites, his eyes meeting Melissa's in amusement before she bit into hers. Finally Casey made his choice and devoured it quickly. She handed him a napkin, so he could wipe the frosting off his face. "If you're thirsty, there's a drinking fountain across the hall," she said.

"Okay." He slid off the chair and left her office.

Travis got to his feet, hardly knowing where to start thanking her for all she'd done. But before he could get a word out she said, "Quick—find your son and go. I'll follow you to the front doors." She picked up the cupcake carton and they left her office, gathering Casey along the way.

"I wish you could have stayed longer," she explained to him, "but I've got another patient waiting for me. Have fun at school." She handed the cupcakes to Travis. "Bye, Casey."

"Bye."

Her brilliant strategy had left his son confused. She'd been right; now was the time to act. Travis walked beside him to the car and they took off for his school, not giving him the luxury of thinking about what had just happened.

"Dad? I want Melissa to go to the movie with us."

Oh, no. He should've known! "She meant you should take one of your friends, Casey. I was thinking Blaine." He was a boy Casey often played with, who lived down the street from them.

"I don't want to go with him. She's more fun!"

She was definitely that. And maybe too clever? Travis wanted to believe the therapist had no ulterior motive when she'd handed him those passes, but he couldn't be sure. If she was interested in him, then this wasn't the first time a woman had tried to get his attention through his child.

Since moving to Utah, he'd met attractive women who'd come on to him, but he'd felt no answering spark and couldn't pretend otherwise. After one date, he couldn't bring himself to repeat the experience.

"We don't have to worry about it now. The passes are good for six months."

"But I want to see *Spider-Man* with her this week before the movie's gone!"

"We'll have to talk about it later." Relieved that the school was in sight, he pulled into the parking lot.

Because Travis had talked with Casey's teacher several times already, she handled the interruption to her morning class like the pro she was. The kids were delighted to get treats, and enough fuss was made of Casey that Travis could slip out before his son could decide he didn't want to stay.

Travis would never have thought of using his son's birthday as a way to get him back to class. But Melissa's tactic was the kind of thing Valerie might have done, and it had worked. He drove straight to the P.I. firm on Wasatch Boulevard, feeling as if he'd just survived a blizzard before reaching the top of Everest.

En route, he rang Deana and told her Casey was back in class, hopefully for the whole day. Travis planned to pick him up, but he would appreciate her staying until they got home, in case something went wrong before the school day was over.

Because of the therapist's clever handling of his son, life looked as if it might be getting back to normal. He was indebted to Melissa and her unorthodox methods. At the same time, he felt conflicted. He knew it wasn't her fault she reminded him of Valerie. And therein lay the problem. She *wasn't* his deceased wife. That woman was gone. More than ever he didn't want to be around her stand-in.

With a groan of frustration, he pressed on the accelerator, anxious to get to his office. What he needed was to dig into a new case, something that kept him physically active so he wouldn't have time to think. Roman had told him that a half-dozen cases he'd probably like were waiting for him. He could choose the one that appealed to him most.

As for Casey, he would have to go to the movie with his father and his eleven-year-old cousin, Jack. Or maybe just the two of them would go. He'd given in to his son's wishes long enough.

ON THURSDAY Melissa rushed inside Rinaldo's at the lunch hour. The place was crowded, but Tom had grabbed a booth and was waiting for her. She walked over and sat down opposite him.

"Sorry I'm late, but my last appointment lasted longer than I'd planned."

"Don't worry about it. I took the liberty of ordering our lunch, since I know you have to get back to work soon."

"I do. Thanks for going ahead. You'll be glad to know I've finished my part of our project." Melissa handed Tom the portfolio containing the artwork she'd done in watercolor for his book.

After the waitress brought their food, she ate while he looked through it. "These are perfect, Melissa."

"I'm glad you're pleased. Go ahead and take it to your office to scan everything before you send it off to your publisher."

"I want to do more than that," he said, with a look of longing in his eyes. "I've got ideas for a whole series of books based on World War II. Take a peek." He opened his briefcase and handed her a proposal he'd put together. "We make a great team."

No. Not in the way he meant. It was code for he wanted to marry her. This had to end now.

"Tom, I'm flattered that you want me to collaborate on your terrific stories, but I'm not interested in doing more of this kind of work."

He stared at her in disbelief. "I can't believe you're serious. You're a wonderful artist."

She'd been afraid of this, but it had to be said. "Thank you so much for giving me the opportunity, but I have my reasons."

"What are they?"

"Well, I've discovered that my work as a therapist keeps me so busy, I don't like the outside stress of deadlines. I've always painted for pleasure and don't want that to change now."

"Surely you realize a lot of money could be involved here—" The mention of money couldn't mask the hurt in his voice.

"I'm not after money," she stated quickly.

"Then it's me you don't like."

"Of course I do, or I wouldn't have worked with you on this."

He seemed to hesitate before he said, "Don't you realize how I feel about you?"

"Oh, Tom. Since my divorce I've been focused on my work. You're in a different place than I am. I love my freedom and don't want that to change." She hated it that he'd gotten emotionally attached without any encouragement from her. For him to have built a romantic fantasy about them was ludicrous. In Melissa's opinion he ought to go back to his wife, but she would never say that. All she could do was be firm.

When he didn't respond she added, "You're the writer and can attract other artists much more talented than I am. I don't doubt that in time you'll meet that special someone."

"Wait," he said, as she put a twenty-dollar bill on the table and got to her feet.

"I can't. I have to get back to the clinic. Let this lunch be on me. Naturally, I'll be available for anything else I have to do before the book goes to publication."

On that note she turned and worked her way through the lunch crowd, doubly thankful she'd never been anything but professional with Tom. He certainly couldn't accuse her of leading him on.

In truth, she'd been distracted by something else since she'd awakened that morning. For some reason she'd expected a phone call from Mr. Stillman, telling her Casey was back to not wanting to go to school. But then she did a rethink. If the little boy pulled another stunt, his dad would most likely go through another avenue to get help, and she would never know how things worked out for him.

For the rest of the afternoon she stayed busy, then left for the gym. A good workout was what she needed; it always helped relieve tension. But when she got home, she still felt at loose ends. She wanted to blame it on the unhappy moments at the restaurant earlier with Tom.

She should have been able to see his real intentions when he'd asked her to collaborate with him. But she didn't blame him. He was only doing what a divorced man would do to move on, and she must have seemed like a perfect start.

Casey's widowed father, on the other hand, wasn't looking. Any woman who hoped to draw the former Texas Ranger's attention was delusional.

In the end, Melissa climbed into bed with a portfolio of some of her old paintings. For years she'd been working on characters that one day might be the inspiration for children's cartoons for the screen. She worked with acrylics, and little by little she felt she was improving. But she hadn't yet achieved something she considered good enough to send to an agent who would approach a film studio for her.

After studying some of her paintings, she set the portfolio aside and began a new sketch.

The next thing she knew, it was morning. When she rolled out of bed, her right foot landed on the sketch pad, which had fallen to the floor at some point in the night. She picked it up and was shocked to discover a familiar face looking back at her.

Casey Stillman. Somehow he had worked his way onto the paper. An older Casey—maybe thirteen— astride an animal with three horns coming through a prehistoric-looking forest. Over his strong body he wore skins, and a thong around his forehead. One hand clutched a spear. His leg carried a jagged scar from thigh to ankle. A teen superhero…

Pleased with the drawing, she sat on the mattress and added a few more touches. Finally satisfied, she removed the sketch from the pad and slid it under the bed.

Later she'd take it to an art store and have it framed. After taking her pad and portfolio to the other bedroom, which she'd set up as a studio, she showered and dressed for work.

Since she would never see Casey again, she was glad she had a memento of him. That little boy must have really gotten to her, showing up in her art as he had.

But as she drove to the clinic a half hour later, she realized she needed to get her mind on other things. Tomorrow being Saturday, she would get up early and drive to the cabin.

Remembering the talk with her parents, she made a mental note to phone her brother, John, and ask him to bring Nedra and the kids for an overnighter. If they couldn't come, she'd call her sister, Linda. Maybe she and Brent would bring their children. Surely one of her siblings would be able to join her. But if no one could make it, Melissa decided, she'd stay till dark before leaving for home, and return on Sunday morning.

It angered her that strangers trespassed with no conscience and made themselves comfortable in a cabin that didn't belong to them. She'd felt violated. And then there was the fact that she'd seen no sign of a break-in. That disturbed her a lot. Someone had a key, or a way to get in, and could walk in on her at any time. She supposed the first thing she could do when she got up there was hunt for John's old baseball bat and keep it with her so she wouldn't feel completely helpless.

Kamas was only thirty miles east of Sandy. They had to drive another two miles on dirt roads to reach their property. The log cabin, built in 1935, was at a higher elevation and somewhat isolated from other cabins in the forest. She could see it made a perfect target for lowlifes—her father's term for people who made themselves at home on someone else's land.

If she found more signs of trespassers using their cabin, she'd tell her parents she was calling the police, and she'd meet them there herself. Something had to be done. The cabin had always been her retreat. It was important.

As soon as she reached the clinic, she made phone calls to her siblings. No one was free this weekend, though John told her he'd get back to her if anything changed. She thanked him, but didn't count on it. So she wouldn't be able to go up to the cabin. Melissa was deflated by that prospect, but knew there was nothing else to do but accept it and immerse herself in work.

Fridays usually turned out to be the busiest day of the week. That was a good thing. She'd barely said goodbye to her first patient when the receptionist told her she had a call on line four. Maybe it was John. She picked up and almost said his name, but caught herself in time. "Melissa Dalton."

"Ms. Dalton?" Her pulse picked up speed when she recognized that baritone voice. "This is Travis Stillman."

"Good morning. How's Casey doing?"

"He's the reason I'm calling." *Uh-oh.* "Would you happen to be free after work today?"

What?

"Casey wants you to go to the movie with us."

"I take it he's weaned himself from the crutches."

"He has, all because of you. He wants to thank you for the birthday treats. I told him you were a very busy lady, but he asked me to try and arrange it. Hopefully it won't interfere with your plans for the evening."

"No, it's a perfect time for me."

"You're through at four-thirty?"

"Yes. I'll meet you at the theater if you'll tell me which one."

"In the Bell Canyon Plaza. It's the latest *Spider-Man*. There's a showing at four forty-five."

"I'll be there."

"We'll meet you outside the box office to give you your ticket."

"Sounds good. Tell Casey thanks for sharing his gift. I'll see you both later."

"Until then."

She hung up, but when she thought about the invitation, her excitement quickly subsided. This had been Casey's doing, not his father's. And just as Melissa had avoided meeting Tom in the evenings, Travis Stillman had arranged this outing during the day.

No mention of picking her up beforehand or eating dinner afterward. He'd even gone so far as to say he didn't want to interfere with her evening plans. That didn't surprise her. The last thing he'd be looking for— if he were looking—would be a woman who reminded him of his wife.

Where Casey was concerned, she had to remember that children could be manipulative. He liked getting presents and it wasn't beyond the realm of possibility that he was hoping to wangle one more out of her. That was why she would show up empty-handed.

Melissa worked through until four-twenty, then left for the movie theater. The minute she climbed out of her Jeep, she heard her name being called. And there was Casey, running up to her. No one would know he'd ever had a broken leg.

His father, striking in a black polo and khakis, stood back with his hands on his hips. She noticed he'd drawn the attention of several women, not just her.

Casey broke into a smile. "That's an awesome Jeep."

"Thanks. I love it."

"I wish I could ride in it sometime."

"Maybe you can. It's up to your father. How's school?" She started walking toward his dad. Casey kept up with her.

"Pretty good. Thanks for the cupcakes."

"You're welcome. Thanks for asking me to come to the movie. After being at work all day, this is a treat." She lifted her gaze to find a pair of midnight-blue eyes staring down at her. They weren't quite as frosty this afternoon, thank goodness. "It's nice to see you again, Mr. Stillman."

"Casey and I are pleased you could come. We'd better go in. The previews have probably started."

He held the main door open for them, and they passed through the lobby to the theater itself. She was careful not to brush against him, but even without touching, she was aware of him. The place wasn't crowded yet, though the previews were on. Casey took the lead and walked down the aisle to an empty row. "Can we sit here?"

"I was just going to pick it," his father said.

Melissa moved ahead so Casey would be sitting between them.

"I'll get us some popcorn and be right back," Travis murmured.

"Thanks, Dad." When he'd gone, Casey turned his head to look at her. "Do you like Spider-Man?"

"I think he's amazing the way he swings around on his web, looking for bad guys."

"Except he's not real. But my dad is."

"What do you mean?"

"He looks for bad guys."

Melissa didn't know what to say to that, for fear she'd bring up something painful. His father might have moved to Utah, but he'd never give up the search for the criminal who'd killed his wife. "You mean a long time ago."

"No, now. He's a P.I. You know—he looks for people doing bad things."

She blinked. Travis Stillman was a private investigator? "Here in Salt Lake?"

"Yup. At Lufka's."

Lufka's? She'd seen that name written somewhere, but not in Casey's patient file. "I didn't know that."

Just as the main feature started, his father returned with a tub of popcorn and passed it down. Throughout the film she munched on it, but her mind wasn't on the film. While Casey sat there totally absorbed, she was thinking about what he'd told her. Until people got up to leave, she didn't even realize the movie was over.

"I wish we could watch it again," Casey said to his dad.

"I know, but we can't. We're due at your aunt Pat's for dinner. Let's go."

Melissa filed out of the row after them. They made their way through the lobby and outside. Without looking at his father, she patted Casey on the shoulder. "Thanks for inviting me. I loved the movie and the popcorn. Now I have to go or I'll be late for my dinner date." In this case she hoped she could be forgiven for a small white lie.

"I wish you could come with us."

"But she can't." His father's voice had an edge. "Have you thanked her for coming?"

Casey's blue eyes revealed a poignant longing that caught her off guard. "Thanks, Melissa."

She smiled. "I bet I had a better time than you did. Have fun at your aunt's. Are you taking Dexter with you?"

He nodded.

"Lucky dog," she said, and hurried off to her Jeep to prevent his father from having to say another word.

Once inside, she reached into her purse for her iPhone and searched for Lufka's in Salt Lake. A list with that spelling came up. She clicked on the first entry, and up popped the website for the Lufka Private Investigator firm on Wasatch Boulevard. Now she remembered where she'd seen it before. She'd passed their place of business hundreds of times.

Her eyes took in the information. The firm covered everything from surveillance and insurance fraud to missing persons, stalking cases, theft of property and protection to individuals. In Melissa's mind, Mr. Stillman had traded one dangerous job for another, and would make an adversary without equal.

Not wasting another second, she headed for her parents' home. She knew they had a business dinner tonight, but maybe they hadn't left yet. Melissa needed to talk to them. She had an idea.

Chapter Three

After dropping Casey off at school Monday morning, Travis drove to work. Despite the promise of another hot, beautiful September day, he was in a foul mood.

As he was getting out of his car, Chaz walked over to him. "Things must be better with Casey or you wouldn't be here." But when he got closer and scrutinized him, he added, "So how come you look like you haven't slept in a week? What's wrong?"

"Let's just say I've been haunted by a ghost."

Chaz frowned. The guys knew about Valerie and had always been sensitive to his moods. "That doesn't sound good. Want to talk about it?"

Travis let out a deep sigh. "Maybe I should." He looked around. Roman wasn't here yet. When his boss arrived, they were going to go over the new missing person's case he'd been assigned. Travis had barely started the groundwork, and had some questions only Roman could answer through his connections with the police department. "Sure you have the time?"

"I'll make it. Come on."

He followed Chaz inside. Somebody had brought SweetSpuds for the staff, probably Mitch. Since marrying Heidi Norris, whose family owned the SweetSpuds doughnut company, Mitch kept them in good supply. Before long they would all have to go on a strict diet, but not this morning.

Travis poured them coffee and took it to Chaz's office, while his friend carried the doughnuts. "You know the therapist Casey saw last week, and then he suddenly had a miraculous recovery?" He sat down heavily in a visitor's chair.

Chaz's eyes narrowed as he settled behind his desk. "Yeah?"

Travis rubbed his face with his hands before letting out a groan. "Weird as this may sound, she looks and acts like…Valerie."

A shadow crept over Chaz's face. "You mean…"

"I mean Melissa Dalton could be her double, in a superficial way, of course. I almost had a heart attack when I met her." His voice grated as he continued, "It hit me so hard, I couldn't respond naturally around her." He drank some coffee, but forgot it was hot, and the liquid scalded his tongue.

"And Casey?"

"I don't even know where to begin."

Chaz leaned forward. "Has he said she reminds him of his mother?"

"No. I think he's afraid to admit it to me, but I'm convinced he's already bonded with her. Since she went to that movie with us on Friday, he's worked himself up into seeing her again. I shouldn't have given in to him. I feared there'd be a price to pay, but the thought of him refusing to go to school drove me to it. I purposely made it for the afternoon and—"

"Travis," Chaz broke in. "I'm confused."

"You're not the only one."

"Try telling me this from the beginning."

He nodded. "Okay. Last Monday, when I took Casey to his first appointment with her, she challenged him to walk without his crutches. Just like that, he put them down and started walking around the therapy room with her. It was amazing. If I hadn't been there to witness it, I wouldn't have believed it."

For the next five minutes Travis unloaded to Chaz. When he'd finished, his friend stared hard at him. "My next question for you is might there be a part of you that wants to see her again?"

"Hell, no!" Travis shot out of the chair and began pacing. If he did want to see her again, he'd need his head examined. "But Casey does."

"How come you're so upset? If you don't want anything more to do with her, then Casey will have to accept it. Even if he goes into another funk for a week or two, that will be the end of it."

Travis sighed. "You're right. I just need to get over the shock. Thanks for talking to me. I'd better get to work. Roman should be here by now."

"Bring Casey over tonight. We've invited Mitch and Heidi. They'll bring Zack. It's still beautiful weather. We're going to grill some hamburgers out on the deck. Lacey and Abby will be thrilled if you two come."

"Thanks, Chaz. I think I'll take you up on that. It'll be fun for Casey. I'll bring the dessert."

His friend smiled. "Not necessary. Just make sure Dexter comes, too. Abby loves him."

"Will do."

Travis headed to Roman's office, feeling better after having aired his fears to Chaz. But he hadn't told him everything. On Friday he'd discovered Melissa Dalton was the only woman of his acquaintance who showed no personal interest in him. He knew it when he couldn't feel any vibes coming from her.

Travis wasn't a vain man, but the few times she'd glanced at him, she'd seemed to look right through him. Their conversation on the phone when he'd told her about Valerie had been brief and to the point. She didn't draw things out or show undue curiosity. Didn't voice the usual platitudes.

Generous as she'd been to Casey, Travis sensed she wouldn't like it if he brought his son around her again. She'd been professional and accommodating to her patient, but there was a limit, and Casey had reached it. *Travis* needed therapy if he allowed this situation to get to him. There was no reason they would ever see each other again. Ships passing in the night.

Roman had arrived, and motioned to him from his office. "Come on in and sit down. I've got something to discuss with you."

"I was just going to ask you a few questions concerning the new case myself."

His boss shook his head. "I've turned it over to Rand." Rand was one of the older P.I.s who'd worked there for several years.

Travis squinted at his boss. "Maybe you didn't realize that Casey is fine now and back in school."

"I heard and it's great news. But something else has come up and your name was mentioned as the person to get the job done. Ever heard of William Roberts?"

"No."

"He's the CEO of the Wasatch Front Steel company."

"*That* name I've heard of."

"Everyone has. Their family is one of the most prominent in our fair city. They've owned property in the Kamas area for close to eighty years, up in the Wasatch-Cache National Forest. The first Roberts settlers erected a cabin in 1935, and it has been used and maintained by the family ever since.

"After the twenty-fourth of July, his daughter went up several times alone and discovered that someone, maybe several people, have been using the cabin on weekdays. She's nervous to go up there at all now, and had a talk with her parents. Mr. Roberts told her he'd look into it the next chance he got.

"Apparently owners of other cabins farther down the mountain have had occasional break-ins too, but the police have told them they can do nothing unless they see a crime in action. To Mr. Roberts's knowledge, nothing in their cabin is missing, but there are definite signs of occupation. He phoned our company to look into the problem and catch the intruders. I talked with him yesterday. He requested you."

Travis was mystified. "Because of another case I've worked on?"

"No. Because you're a former Texas Ranger. It seems

his daughter has met you and learned you're now a P.I. She recommended you to her father and he called me."

The hairs stood up on the back of Travis's neck. "What's her name?"

"Melissa Dalton. Does it ring a bell?"

The news brought him to his feet. With a different last name, it meant she was either divorced or widowed. It would explain the absence of a ring on her finger, and her dinner date for Friday night. At the time he'd wondered if she didn't wear rings because she did a lot of physical therapy with children.

After concluding that she had *no* interest in him, Travis found, his thoughts going through a 180-degree reversal. He'd never told her that he worked as a P.I. now. The subject hadn't come up. Which meant she must have learned it through Casey.

Travis thought back to last week. The only time the two of them were alone was at the movie, when he'd gone out to buy popcorn. Had she asked Casey questions out of curiosity? Or had his boy just been chatty and told her the story of his life in those five minutes?

What kind of work Travis did since they'd moved from Texas wasn't a secret. But with Valerie's killer still on the loose, everyone kept quiet about his former occupation. For her of all people to find out, and then go to her father, came as a big surprise. Knowing how she felt—or didn't feel—about him made it an even bigger one.

"What's going on, Travis? This woman obviously means something to you."

Roman's question jerked him out of his thoughts. He

glanced at him. "She's the therapist who worked with Casey last week."

His boss smiled. Travis didn't miss the twinkle in his eyes. "Whatever went on, nice job."

"Nothing went on." Roman could be a terrible tease.

"Whatever you say." His boss stood up and handed him the new file. "Her cell phone number is in there, along with the notes I took. Mr. Roberts wants you to work with his daughter. She's the one who uses the cabin the most, and can tell you everything you need to know.

"He's made phone calls to his neighbors and indicated that a lot of well-heeled cabin owners up there will be indebted to you. The list is included. They're willing to pay any amount to get rid of the trespassers, and want you to start today."

"After that buildup, I guess I don't have a choice."

"There's always a choice. You know that." Roman had more integrity than anyone he knew. "Say the word and I'll give it to Rand."

Travis broke out in a cold sweat. This was a dilemma he could never have anticipated. But as long as Casey didn't know about it, and Travis kept any contact with Melissa Dalton to a minimum, he supposed it could work. "Today, you say?"

Roman nodded. "Gather your crew. Anything you need, just let me know. Jose and Lon are available for backup. Adam's on another case, but should be finished shortly."

Jose was ex-FBI with the Bureau of Alcohol, Tobacco and Firearms, and had worked for years on assignments in Latin America. Lon was a retired police chief who'd once headed the Salt Lake City SWAT team. Both were great resources among the many operatives Roman employed. Travis liked working with them when they were available. "That's good to know. Okay, I'm out of here."

"Keep me posted, comrade."

Travis chuckled. Because of his Russian heritage, Roman often put in an exaggerated accent when he spoke to the guys. He was a bit of a joker.

The first thing Travis needed to do was let Deana know not to fix dinner, because he and Casey were going to Chaz and Lacey's.

Next, he dipped into the file Roman had given him. After finding Melissa's cell number, he programmed it and the clinic number into his iPhone, then went out to the firm's shop to gather batteries, surveillance cameras and a listening device.

Everything for the staff's use was stored in there. Roman's brother, Yuri, manufactured electronic gadgets and sent them out from the East Coast for the firm to try out. The place was a gold mine for the latest state-of-the-art equipment. Sometimes Yuri flew out with his family. He was an even bigger tease than Roman. The two brothers were so entertaining, everyone flocked around.

Travis wore a smile out to the car, but once inside, he felt the reality of the situation hit home. *Just call her and get it over with, Stillman.*

Gripping his cell, he phoned the clinic and left a message with the receptionist for Melissa Dalton to call him ASAP. He needed a key to her family's cabin, and directions. If he didn't hear from her within the hour, he'd try her cell. With that accomplished, he headed for home to change clothes and load his truck.

MELISSA HAD JUST TAKEN a shower and was eating toast in the kitchen when her cell phone rang. Her heart kicked, which surprised her. It hadn't done that in years.

She checked the caller ID, wondering if it might be Travis Stillman. On Sunday her father had talked to the owner of the Lufka firm and had hired them, specifically Mr. Stillman, to check in to the problem at the cabin. But Casey's dad might be in the middle of another case and one of the other P.I.s would have to be assigned.

Even if Casey's father had been available, he might have declined taking the case when he found out Melissa had been the one to suggest him for the job. Then she would know in a hurry he preferred to have no more contact with her. Whether it was because she reminded him of his wife or some other reason, she would have to let it go. It surprised her that she even cared.

When she saw the clinic's number on her caller ID, she felt a double spasm of disappointment before picking up. Why were they phoning when she'd taken the day off?

"This is Melissa."

"Hi. It's Susan. Sorry to bother you at home, but Mr. Stillman just called the clinic and asked if you would phone him right back. It sounded important. Here's his number."

Melissa ran over to the counter where she kept a pad

and pencil and wrote it down. To her frustration, she saw her hand was unsteady. "Thanks, Susan."

After she clicked off, she phoned Casey's father, taking several calming breaths while she waited for him to pick up.

"Ms. Dalton?"

"Yes."

"I appreciate your calling me back so fast, but I didn't expect your receptionist to interrupt one of your therapy sessions."

"She didn't. I'm at home."

He was quiet for a second. "You're not ill, I hope."

"No. Nothing like that. I took the day off when my father told me he'd hired your firm. He wants me to be available for you."

"I see. Casey must have told you about my work."

"When he explained that Spider-Man caught bad guys, he also mentioned that you look for bad guys 'for real.' I asked him what he meant and he told me you were a P.I. who worked for Lufka's. I looked it up on the internet and found the website. When I saw the word *surveillance,* I thought it an amazing coincidence." She was talking too fast, but couldn't seem to stop herself.

"In what way?"

"Ever since the July 24 holiday, I've been entertaining the idea of hiring somebody to find out who's invading our cabin when we're not there. I told Dad I'd be willing to help pay for a retired police officer to stay at the cabin until winter. He said he'd try talking to the police again, but I feared we'd get nowhere there."

"I heard about that from my boss this morning," Travis replied. "Roman Lufka talked to your father, who told him you've got a problem up there. I've agreed to look into it, and understand you're the one who can help me get started."

She leaned against the counter, trying to recover from her adrenaline rush. "I didn't know if you'd be involved in another case, but I thought we should ask for you just the same."

"Actually, I'd been assigned to a missing person's case, but my boss took me off it after talking to your father. It's the least I can do after you helped my son realize he didn't need those crutches. You have a way with children, Ms. Dalton."

"Thank you. But would you please call me Melissa?"

"Okay, and you call me Travis."

"I will. We're very grateful to you. I, most of all, since I'm the one who spends a lot of time up there. Fall is one of the most beautiful seasons in the woods. I'm really angry about what's happened. We've been invaded."

"You have every right to be upset. Since you're free, I'll come by for you now and we'll drive up there."

"We can take my Jeep."

"Except that it will be familiar to the culprits if they've been watching your comings and goings."

Melissa shivered at the idea. "You're right."

"My truck won't raise suspicions. If you have any maps of the area, bring them."

"We have a drawer full of U.S. Geological Survey maps at the cabin. My brother pores over them at every opportunity."

"That's even better. I want to see everything inside and out. We'll come home in time for me to drop you off and pick up Casey after school. By then I'll have a much better idea of how I want to handle your case."

"I'll be ready in five minutes."

"Good. I've loaded some food and drinks in my backpack. When we reach Kamas, I'd like to go on foot from there. I understand your cabin is only a couple of miles up the mountain."

"That's right." Hiking was one of her favorite things to do in this world. Waves of delight swept through her. A picnic with a Texas Ranger among the wildflowers would be like something out of a fantasy. With him around, no way could she get hurt.

The biggest problem for her would be remembering it was only a dream. When he'd solved the case, the dream would be over.

"Give me your address." When she'd done his bidding, he told her he'd be there in ten minutes. Then he rang off.

She hurried upstairs to the bedroom and removed her robe, choosing to wear jeans and a peach-colored T-shirt. After putting on her hiking boots, she went into the bathroom to do her hair. If they were going to be doing a lot of hiking, she preferred it off her neck, and opted for a French twist, using a couple of inlaid-wood hair sticks.

After applying a liberal coating of sunscreen, she put the tube in one of her back pockets with apricot-frost lipstick. In the other one she stashed her keys and a twenty-dollar bill. That was all she needed. She kept a lot of art supplies at the cabin. In fact, her bedroom there looked like a painting studio. If time permitted, she'd do some drawings.

When she was ready, she went downstairs and grabbed two cold apples from the fridge. He might like one. Making sure the lights were off, she locked the door behind her and walked out to the drive to wait for him. She hadn't taken a day off in a long time. It was almost like being a kid again playing hooky.

Melissa was feeling so good she feared her latent divorcée hormones had finally decided to kick in. Until now she'd thought the whole idea was a myth.

A few neighbors waved on their way to the carport. No doubt they were surprised to see her out in front eating an apple as if she didn't have a care in the world. In another minute a steel-green metallic Silverado four-door truck pulled into the driveway with Travis at the wheel. She ran around to the passenger side and climbed in so he wouldn't have to get out and help her.

On a scale of one to ten, one being the most like the frozen Arctic, she decided the blue eyes that met hers were probably closer to a thawed-out four. The vast improvement lifted her spirits. If he'd really been turned off by her, he wouldn't have considered taking this case, no matter what his boss wanted.

"I brought you an apple, but if you don't want it, that's fine."

"Thanks." He took it from her and bit into it, studying her at the same time from head to toe until she was almost suffocated from inner heat. The way she'd done her hair seemed to fascinate him. If his wife had worn it this way, Melissa didn't want to know about it.

"You don't have a purse," he said. "Do you want to go back for it?"

She shook her head. "I have everything I need in my pockets."

"Incredible," he muttered. In the next instant he looked around and backed out to the street. Then they took off. Like her, he'd dressed in jeans and a T-shirt, but every inch of him was hard lines and sinew. Out of the corner of her eye she saw his backpack lying on the seat behind him.

"Have you been to Kamas before, Travis?"

"No, but I drove up Parley's Canyon to Park City to ski with some coworkers several times last winter."

"Those places aren't far apart. Our cabin is two miles beyond the town, farther up in the forest, at 8,500 feet."

He finished the apple and tossed the core with hers into the plastic bag he used for waste. "I thought the Davis Mountains of West Texas were amazing until I came here and saw the Uintas."

"All mountains have their own beauty. Unfortunately, there are lawless people who ruin it for everyone else." When he didn't say anything, she glanced at him and saw that his jaw with its dark shadow had hardened. "I—I'm sorry if what I said brought back your pain," she stammered.

"Don't worry about it. I've been living with pain for a long time. Because of Casey, I'm able to deal with my wife's death."

"I know what you mean. The children I work with

brought me out of my depression after my divorce. When they're around, you have to meet their needs. In the process, you forget yourself."

"Yup. The day my wife was buried, I wanted to crawl into the ground with her. Then Casey whispered that he didn't feel good and needed to go the bathroom."

In spite of her sorrow for Travis, Melissa laughed gently. "The day I received my divorce decree, one of my young patients caught me crying. She asked me what was wrong. Not thinking, I told her my marriage was over. She said, 'You're lucky. Now you get to sleep with your mommy.'"

Unexpected laughter burst out of Travis. It gave her a glimpse into that hidden part of him. She was pretty sure he was a man who'd once laughed a lot. How would it be to get to know *that* man...?

"Have you been divorced for a while?"

"Six years."

"You must have been a child bride."

"Being married at twenty-one does sound young these days. To make it worse, I was married to a child groom." One who was Dr. Jekyll to everyone else, but when they were alone, he became a version of Mr. Hyde, who watched and knew every move she made until she couldn't breathe.

"How long did it last?"

"Seven months."

"I'm sorry."

"I'm not. It wasn't meant to be. You know those boxes you have to check as the primary reason for the divorce?"

He nodded.

"Well," she continued, "instead of 'incompatibility,' the first one ought to read 'total and complete immaturity.'"

Her comment produced another laugh from him.

"I can laugh about it now, too," she said.

She actually could laugh about that part of it, but the other part... Russ's dark side... She'd since learned that he'd married again and moved to California. The news had made her euphoric, but if she ever allowed herself to think about it, she trembled for his unsuspecting wife.

"You know, I wish I could find that little girl again and tell her I didn't end up sleeping with my mommy, but I'm a lot happier now."

Melissa looked out the side window, knowing Travis couldn't say the same thing. Even if his wife's killer were caught and given the death penalty, it wouldn't undo the pain of losing her. The horrific murder had robbed Casey of his mother. Melissa heaved a sigh. It was all too sad, but to wallow in it wouldn't do either of them any good.

"I have several theories about the people breaking into the cabin," she said without preamble. "The first one is that they're probably deer hunters without permits, checking out their favorite spots ahead of time and using the cabin as their motel."

His lips twitched. "That's a possibility."

"The second one is that a couple of unemployed high school dropouts wanted by the police are hanging out where no one can find them."

"I like that one."

Apparently she was amusing him, but this was better than dwelling on his tragic past. "The third one is kind of outside-the-box thinking."

"Go on. I'm intrigued."

"A Sasquatch family has decided our cabin is the perfect retreat."

Again, laughter rumbled out of him. When it subsided he said, "Don't tell me. You're a regular listener of the *Stargazer Paranormal* radio show."

"I used to be, but the host was replaced so I don't listen anymore."

"You liked Lacey Pomeroy?"

Her eyes widened. "Did you used to listen to her show, too?"

"A couple of times."

"Ooh, I wish she hadn't gone off the air. Sometimes I work late and I loved to hear her talk about other worlds."

"Rumor has it she got married and retired into a life of obscurity."

"I figured it had to be something like that, but it's my loss."

Travis flashed her a glance. "Does this mean you do a night clinic?"

"No. I paint."

His gaze roved over her with new interest. "Am I in the presence of a famous artist?"

It was her turn to laugh. "I just play at it for my own pleasure." She could get lost in it, the best kind of therapy to rid herself of past demons.

He slowed down to make a turn. They'd be in Kamas soon. "The art hanging in your office—it's yours?"

"Yes."

"Why didn't you sign them?" He sounded surprised. "You're very good."

He sounded as if he meant it. "Thank you. Lest you think I'm crazy for putting up my own stuff and letting my art remain anonymous, I have my reasons."

"You mean besides making your office a place children love to visit? Casey said he wished he could take home that picture of the superhero sleeping against the huge bulldog."

"He did?" That pleased her. "I painted that soon after my bulldog died." She'd mourned the loss of him extra hard.

"But he had four legs."

The man sitting next to her didn't miss anything. When law enforcement failed, you called in a Texas Ranger to get the job done. She'd heard that all her life and couldn't believe she was actually sitting next to one.

"My bulldog, Spike, was my *second* dog."

"Spike?"

"Like the dog in the Tom and Jerry comics."

"I liked those old cartoons. Still do."

With those words, her feelings warmed toward him. "So do I. Anyway, it was my first dog, Cleo, who was missing a leg. She was a white Bichon. A real cutie. She was a happy little thing, quite unaware she had only three legs."

"Do you have a dog now?"

"No. With the hours I keep, it would be alone too much."

"I know what you mean. We have a part-time house-keeper who watches out for Dexter."

"A housekeeper who cleans and cooks is what *I* need, so I can have more time to spend on my hobby."

She felt him glance at her. "Lest I think you're crazy for exhibiting your talent in public, tell me your real reason for putting it up in your office."

His brain was a steel trap.

"Okay. One day I'd like to submit my art to a film company that makes animated cartoons. In the mean-time I've brought my art to the office and mounted it, watching to see which samples appeal the most to my patients. But so far I've received such a wide range of responses, I can't decide which pieces would be the best to send to an agent who'll represent me."

She thought of her picture of Casey. If she dared put it up, she'd be fascinated to see if her patients found it more interesting than the others. But now wasn't the time to think about that. Melissa turned her head to-ward Travis, needing to change the subject. "What are some of your ideas about the cabin break-in?" Then she corrected herself. "I suppose I shouldn't say *break-in*— there's no sign of a forced entry."

His expression sobered. "Doesn't matter how they got in. After tracking criminals since my early twen-ties, I had quite a few scenarios springing to mind. But until I pick up some kind of evidence, I'm keeping the many possibilities open to investigation."

"That was a good nonanswer." She said it with a smile.

He shot her an amused glance. "We're coming into Kamas. Let's grab a bite at that fast-food place up ahead."

"You mean Grampy's. They used to make awesome hamburgers, but they're under new management. I hope the food's still good."

"We'll find out. After that I'll drive to a church parking lot to leave the truck and we'll head out on foot."

"Why a church parking lot?"

"They're usually safe places. Anyone looking to hot-wire it, *if* they can open the door, will think twice about stealing it. There's usually a custodian around who could walk out at any time and catch them."

"That makes sense."

He pulled off the road next to some other cars parked in front of Grampy's, where they had to get out to be served. She opened the cab door and jumped down to get in line behind half a dozen other people. Travis followed. In a minute it was their turn.

Melissa knew just about everyone who ran the businesses in town. But she didn't recognize the dark blond employee manning the window. Probably mid-forties, he had a buzz cut and a deeply burnished complexion, with that leathery kind of skin normally seen on a sailor or a beachcomber.

She likely wouldn't have noticed details about him if he hadn't given her that blatant kind of once-over some guys did. Closer now, she saw a glazed look in his eyes.

For a second it reminded her of Russ's crazed expression before he'd struck her.

This man didn't stop staring until Travis moved behind her. Then his gaze turned away to Travis, who didn't need a Texas Ranger uniform to be formidable. Melissa was thankful he was with her.

"What can I get for you and the wife?" The question didn't fool her. Neither she nor Travis wore wedding rings.

She leaned inside the window. "Is that your *wife* cooking back there?"

He glanced at the older woman at the grill, giving Melissa a glimpse of a tattoo on the back of his neck. "I don't have a wife." Melissa could tell that her question had angered him.

"I see," she said. "Well, as it happens, I don't have a husband. Now, I'll have a burger and fries to go. Heavy on the onions."

She pulled out her twenty-dollar bill and plunked it down in front of him. People in the line behind them must have heard her, for they started chuckling. She wasn't sorry. The man had disgusted her. He stood there with spots of anger on his cheeks. The spots went even darker by the time he'd waited on Travis and handed him his order.

By tacit agreement they took their food to a picnic table around the side of the building.

Chapter Four

Travis hadn't liked the way the other man had looked at Melissa. And when his shifty eyes had seen Travis, the way he'd tried to cover up. A woman as pretty as Melissa would always be a target, but there was more to it than that. After chasing down criminals for years, Travis had a gut instinct about them, and this man's behavior put up a red flag.

Obviously, Melissa had seen that look, too—she'd paled in reaction—but she'd camouflaged it by turning the tables on the man. But something had gone on inside her, and Travis planned to get to the bottom of it. He'd wait until she was ready to talk.

Melissa had been a constant surprise from the first moment she'd connected with Casey. Travis might have a problem getting past the similarities to Valerie, yet on the drive up the canyon, he'd enjoyed talking to Melissa, and recognized she was her own person.

Now she sat across from him and tucked into her burger and fries. He wondered how long it would be before they resumed conversation. Before long he'd finished his food, noticing she had, too. "If you're through, shall we drive to the church we passed?"

Her head lifted. "I don't usually behave that rudely to people, even if they deserve it."

He got up and threw their sacks in the receptacle. "The man *did* make a false assumption."

"You mean after he'd—"

"That, too." Travis broke in, reading her mind. "You were certainly within your rights."

"Well, things like that happen often enough." Travis didn't doubt it. "He just happened to pick on the wrong man and woman today."

Curious, Travis cocked his head. "Wrong man?"

"Because of my resemblance to your deceased wife. You must have hated the reminder."

Ah. Now he understood part of her reaction, but not all. She jumped up from the bench and started toward the truck. After they were both in the cab, he angled his head toward her. "Actually, it was probably the first time since her death Valerie wasn't on my mind, but I appreciate your sensitivity. Don't give it another thought."

The more he was getting to know Melissa, the more he realized how different she was from his wife. Since they'd be working together for a while, he needed to get over it. He started the truck and they drove down the street to the church. "How long ago did new management take over there?"

"Around the first of July. Why?"

"Have you noticed any other changes? New people in town?"

"You mean like teens who work here for the summer?"

"That and anything else you find unusual."

"Not really. Normally, I drive straight through to the cabin. But I have to admit that man gave me the creeps."

"You actually went pale."

She jerked her head toward him. "I did?" she asked in an anxious tone. That made him even more suspicious.

He nodded. "What would make you do that?"

"I have no idea."

He knew she was lying.

"Have you ever seen him before?"

"Never. He certainly has no social skills."

Travis agreed. "Do me a favor. Until I've had a chance to take a look around Kamas, don't go to Grampy's for a while." He was afraid Melissa could have made an enemy without realizing it.

"I wouldn't dream of it. Something wasn't right about him."

Amen. Travis would get the whole story out of her later.

He parked in the church lot, where the truck could be seen from the main street. He grabbed his backpack, and once the vehicle was locked they headed out of town and began the ascent to her cabin.

She flashed him a smile free of her earlier tension. "We'll keep heading up this road. It's not that far."

"I'm not complaining." She was entertaining, as well as incredibly beautiful. He took some invigorating breaths of fresh air.

Everywhere he looked, the quaking aspen showed some yellow. Signs of fall were creeping into the landscape. He saw a smattering of orange in various areas, but it would be another month before the heavy mountain foliage would turn into full autumn splendor. With the air still warm and a hot sun shining overhead, Travis felt a sudden infusion of well-being.

Maybe it was being out in nature again, but as they gained in elevation and he used leg muscles that had needed a workout, he found himself thinking he was glad to be alive. He couldn't remember feeling like this in a long time.

He glanced at Melissa. She was keeping right up with him.

"How do you stay in such great shape, Melissa?"

"I usually go to the gym after work."

"It shows. I'm probably holding you back."

She responded with a laugh that said his comment was absurd. He liked it that she didn't take herself too seriously. "You can see a few cabins here and there, but the higher we get, the more isolated things are."

"And more magnificent."

She spread her arms and whirled in a circle. "It is!"

Amused by her behavior, he said, "You sound happy."

"I am, and you're the reason. Since midsummer I've been nervous being up here alone, but today I've got you with me. Casey told me you go after bad people. I'm counting on you to find out what's going on up here."

"I'll do my best."

"That's good enough for me. The cabin is around the next curve in the road." She picked up speed, forcing him to move faster. In a few more minutes he saw the medium-size two-story log cabin half hidden by trees. Tons of pine needles and cones covered the ground. A lot of family life had been lived up here. He spotted an old swing and furniture on the front porch. There was a rope swing hanging from a nearby tree.

The branches of one enormous pine brushed against the eaves. Any agile person could climb the tree and get in an upstairs window using the right device. No glass would have to be broken. Two squirrels chattered noisily, then darted across the sun-dappled roof.

"Aren't they cute?" Melissa said in a quiet voice.

Travis smiled. "I recognize them from several of your paintings." They drew closer. "Before we go inside, I want to walk around and check all the windows and doors from the outside." He looked at the ground. "When you or your family come up, do you always park here in front?"

"Yes. There's no other place for cars."

With further inspection he could see what she meant. Foliage grew too close to the cabin for a vehicle to drive around it. "I see track marks."

"Those are mine."

"All of them? You always come in the Jeep?"

"Yes."

He walked over by some trees. "There's another set of tracks here that have dried since the last rainstorm. They don't match your Jeep tracks."

For a few minutes he took pictures and measurements. He felt her interest as he got out some material to powder the most prominent of the tracks, then lifted it with tape. "I'll drop this off at the lab. In time it might tell us something useful."

Melissa stuck with him as he moved around, trying to open the ground-floor windows. They didn't give way. At the back of the house he noticed cigarette butts leading from the back door into the forest. They were embedded in the dirt and pine needles. In some cases they were ground in.

"Does anyone in your family smoke?"

"No."

He pulled out a pair of disposable gloves and a plastic bag from his pack. After hunkering down, he retrieved what he could. There were enough butts to convince him more than one person had been here.

"I've never noticed those before!" Melissa exclaimed. "I have no idea how fresh they are."

"The forensics lab will run a test and let us know the approximate age and make." He zipped the bag and stowed it in his pack before walking to the back door. When he tried the handle, the lock seemed solid, but again, someone with special tools could open it. "Have you been in and out of this door recently?"

"Not since I realized it could be dangerous. But the last time I was here, I did notice dirt on the floor right inside and left it to show the police."

"Good thinking. I'll check for that in a few minutes." He made the full round of the cabin's exterior before asking her to unlock the front door. "Don't touch anything. When we go inside, what I'd like you to do is point out the items you've noticed that have been moved or disturbed over the last month. I might be able to get some fingerprints."

"Oh…okay."

He put on a fresh pair of gloves. For the next hour he followed her around, finding objects and surfaces to dust. The cabin had a straightforward floor plan. Two bedrooms and a bathroom upstairs, and on the ground floor two more bedrooms, a bathroom, a family room with a fireplace and comfortable furnishings, and a kitchen with a pine picnic table and benches. All very cozy.

With painstaking care Travis lifted the prints he'd found and put the tapes into bags. "So far, so good."

They'd finished in the kitchen where he'd gone through shelves and drawers. His gaze swerved to her smoky-blue eyes, watching his every move. "You have a very inviting cabin and it's…fairly secure."

"In other words, a child could get in with the right tools."

He chuckled. "Afraid so. Anyone wanting in here is a professional, and probably had a key made to the back door. Since I didn't find any cigarette butts in front of the cabin, it stands to reason they've chosen the rear entry, so they won't be seen from the road."

"You think there's more than one person?"

"Maybe three or four." She stood close enough to him that Travis felt the shudder that passed through her body. "My hunch is they've come on foot through the forest. Maybe they're the hunters, teenagers or the Sasquatch family you mentioned."

She smiled. "So what do *you* think?"

Now that he'd given himself permission to look at her, he wondered if he was more attracted to her than to other women because of the resemblance to Valerie. If so, did it matter?

Hell, yes. While they'd been moving around the

cabin, his mind should have been on the task, yet he'd imagined sliding his arms around her supple waist from behind and kissing the side of her neck the way he used to do with Valerie. And that was just for starters.

He was as bad as the letch at Grampy's. Worse even, because her father had hired him to find out who was trespassing on their property, and Melissa trusted him.

In frustration he reached for his pack and pulled out the mini cameras. "It's too early to tell. You say you come up on weekends, but so far you've never seen anyone hiding inside. I have to assume they only come after dark, on week nights. While I was gathering the dirt samples, I found some residue I didn't recognize mixed in, and I want to have it analyzed.

"In the meantime I'll install these cameras around and we'll get pictures on tape. One in the kitchen and one at the back door. Another I'll put at the top of the stairs. I'm also going to plant this listening device in the geranium pot on the kitchen table. The recorder will catch any conversation. "

"What if they notice?" She stayed with him and handed him things he needed.

"I doubt they will. You told me they've been coming around since Pioneer Day. Now that it's September and they haven't been caught or scared off, they feel safe and aren't looking for a trap."

He'd come up tomorrow morning and see if anything incriminating had shown up on the surveillance tapes. Maybe he'd get lucky and find some new cigarette butts and traces of anything else the intruders might have left outside. The garbage can out back hadn't revealed anything.

Except for the cigarette butts, Travis had to admit they'd been careful. No incriminating papers or wrappers in the wastebaskets or closets. Nothing had been hidden in the cushions or under the mattresses. Someone had been careful. Too careful for amateurs.

She cast him a questioning glance. "Does that mean you're through for now?"

It sounded as if she didn't want to leave. "I saw all your art supplies in the upstairs bedroom. You probably wanted to do some painting. But I'd prefer we go now, in case someone's scouting around to make sure it's all clear for tonight. I'm sorry."

"Please don't be. I'm grateful to you for agreeing to solve this nightmare. Our whole family is," she added.

Her pleasant disposition was one of the many remarkable things about her. "That's nice to hear. You can do some painting the next time you're able to come with me."

"I'm free anytime."

That news came as a revelation. "What about your work at the clinic? I don't understand."

"Today is the official beginning of my week's vacation. I take a week off every fall around this time of year, and another one in late spring when the wildflowers are in bloom."

Travis grabbed an extra breath. A whole week with her... "I can see why. The scenery up here is breathtaking." Including her.

He started across the family room. "We'll leave

through the front door and head down to town, looking like two hikers out enjoying the sunshine."

On the way back they drank from the water bottles he'd brought. She shared a granola bar with him and he experienced a period of contentment with her that had been foreign to him for too long.

Closer to town, a car drove past them. Melissa knew the couple, but they weren't neighbors who'd noticed anything disturbed or missing at their place. She provided an invaluable service to Travis by pointing out other cabins and the names of the owners. It all helped him put a picture together.

"How many cabins are above yours?"

"None. Ours is the highest one on this ridge. There's nothing else but forest."

Travis planned to go exploring tomorrow when he came back up, but now he realized he wouldn't be alone. "We've accomplished what I wanted, in time to get you home before I pick up Casey."

She darted Travis a glance. "Is he liking school?"

"I think so. He hasn't pulled a 'sore leg' on me yet." But his son had been plaguing him to go to another movie with Melissa. Before school that morning he'd asked if she could come over to see him walk Dexter with his new leash. Travis had muttered something unintelligible and told him they needed to get going or they'd both be late.

"That's a good sign."

"I live in hope for the peace to continue." At least in that department. But Travis feared his son wasn't about to give up on seeing Melissa again.

She laughed as they made their way back to the church. "Lo and behold, your truck is still here."

"So it is."

After he'd helped her inside, she pulled out her key ring. "I better give this to you now before I forget. It's an extra key to the cabin so you can come and go as you please." She handed it to him, and their fingers brushed. As if he'd just come in contact with a strong electric current, heat snaked up his arm.

It had happened earlier, too, when she'd held the tools he'd needed while he'd installed the cameras. Each time she'd handed him something, the friction of skin against skin had caused him to grow more aware of her.

MELISSA PUT THE KEY RING back in her pocket, but the tingling sensation from his touch was more intense than it had been inside the cabin while she'd been helping him. Something was wrong with her if she could still feel him in every cell of her body.

How embarrassing if he knew it.

Of course he knew it!

Travis Stillman was an extraordinary man who saw and sensed everything. *And she was a nitwit!*

On the way down the canyon, her cell rang. She checked the caller ID. It was Tom. If this had to do with her artwork, Melissa figured she'd better take the call. "Tom?" In the periphery she felt Travis's eyes on her, disturbing her concentration.

"Hi. I'm sorry to bother you. The receptionist at the clinic said you were off today, so I thought I'd take my chances on reaching you at home."

"Actually, I'm out of town. Are you calling because you heard from your editor?"

"Yes. I'm pretty excited. He's accepted everything and wants to be absolutely certain you won't be doing any more artwork. I sent him my ideas for my new series and he likes them. If you were going to be the artist on them as well, he would add some information about it in your bio in the first book."

The man didn't give up. "I'm positive, Tom, but I appreciate you telling me."

"Just checking in case you'd changed your mind."

"I'm afraid not, but congratulations. I'm very happy for you."

"You deserve the same congratulations. Your artwork helped sell it."

"Thanks, Tom. I'm sure we'll be talking again soon. Now I have to run."

No sooner had she hung up than Travis's phone rang. After he checked to see who was calling, his dark brows furrowed and he clicked on. A few seconds later he said, "I'll be there in five minutes," and clicked off.

"Problems at work?" she asked.

"No." She heard him draw in a swift breath, saw his face drain of color. "It was the school calling. Casey fell from the monkey bars at afternoon recess and is complaining of pain. They've got him in the office."

Her stomach clenched in reaction, but she didn't want to show her alarm in front of him. "Then I'm sure he's fine or they would have called an ambulance," she said. "Kids get hurt at school all the time."

His hands gripped the steering wheel so tightly his

knuckles were white. "Not one who's barely mended from a broken leg."

Travis had always appeared in control in her presence, but this was his precious son who was hurt again, and he'd already lost his wife. "I'll come with you and check him out. If need be, we'll drive him to the clinic and take an X-ray. The radiologist will tell you if you need to talk to his surgeon."

"You don't mind?" he asked.

"This is what I do all day long at work. It's nice that Casey already knows me, so he won't be as frightened." Not as frightened as his father.

Before long they rolled into the school parking lot. Melissa jumped down the second he'd pulled to a stop, and they hurried inside to reach the main office. Casey saw both of them come into the reception room. His blue eyes widened before he slid off the chair. "Dad… Melissa…"

"Hi, Casey," she said. "I heard you got hurt so I came with your dad to see how you're doing."

His face broke out in a smile. "I fell off the monkey bars and got hurt, but it's feeling a little better now."

Travis hunkered down in front of his son and gave him a hug. "I thought you hurt your leg."

"No, my arm. See?"

Melissa leaned over to inspect the sand burn below his elbow. He moved his arm just fine. No fractures there.

"Ooh," she said. "I bet that stung. But better your arm than your leg."

He nodded. "It really hurt."

"Like I told you before, you're tough, and now you've got a mark of bravery to show for it. I think this calls for ice cream. Don't you, Dad?"

If she didn't know better, she would say Travis was in a state of shock. If he'd stayed on the phone long enough, he might have heard a whole explanation from the receptionist and saved himself all this angst. But it showed his love for his son, and she found that trait in this tough man completely endearing.

Travis got to his feet, his color slowly returning. "Let's go, shall we?"

"Yeah." Casey turned to the receptionist. "Thanks for calling my dad."

"Anytime. Glad to see you're fine now." She winked at Travis and gave Melissa a smile before the three of them walked out to the truck.

"Can we go to Farr's?" He'd climbed in the back and fastened his seat belt. "They'll put M&M's in my ice cream."

"I like candy in my ice cream, too," Melissa said. "Peppermint is my favorite."

"Dad doesn't like pieces in his."

"Is that so." She flicked her gaze to Travis. "Are you a chocolate man?"

"Yup," Casey answered for his father. "How did you know?"

"A wild guess."

Travis shifted gears. "Melissa's pretty smart."

"I know."

She wore a smile on her face the whole time they visited the ice cream shop. Casey showed his sore arm to the salesgirl, who put extra candies on his ice cream. They all thanked her warmly.

On the way home Casey said, "She sure was nice." He glanced at Melissa. "Can you come to our house and see Dexter?"

Melissa knew what his father wanted her to say. "Do you know, I'd like that, but I have other plans I can't break. Thank you so much, though." Deep down she wanted to go to his house more than anything, but she didn't dare take advantage of the situation.

"Can you come tomorrow?"

By now Travis had pulled the truck in front of her town house. "Melissa will be busy."

"Oh."

"We'll make arrangements for that another time."

"Okay." But he sounded downhearted.

She opened the door. "When you get home, be sure and put some disinfectant on your arm."

His head whipped around to his father. "Do we have any?"

"I'm not sure. If we don't, I'll buy some."

"But it will hurt."

Melissa had an idea. "If you'll wait just a moment, I'll get some for you that doesn't sting." Leaving the truck door open, she darted into her condo. Once inside, she grabbed the can off her bathroom shelf and in seconds was back. Casey had opened his door and undone his seat belt, and now he waited for her on the end of the seat.

"Can you stick out your arm? This is a spray. It'll feel

cool." He nervously extended it. She pressed the nozzle and covered the long scrape with the mist.

"Hey! That didn't even hurt!"

"Nope, and now you're going to be good as new. I'm very proud of you."

Without warning, he reached out and gave her a hug. Luckily, she'd been standing right next to the seat. She hugged him back, then stepped away and shut the door. Her gaze flicked to his father. "See ya," she said, not daring to prolong this. She'd taken her cue from Travis.

"I'll be in touch about tomorrow," he assured her.

"See ya soon!" Casey exclaimed.

She chuckled as she walked back inside. Kids. They never gave up when they wanted something. She was crazy about them, but her feelings for Casey were growing deeper. Naturally, the loss of his mother had a lot to with her desire to comfort him, but that wasn't the only reason.

He was an endearing child in his own right. Fun to talk to. Bright, adorable. A son his father loved with a fierceness she'd noticed from the start. Casey was the reason Travis got up in the morning. She could see why, and she envied him.

After checking her mailbox, she let herself inside the condo without looking back. Because of their hike in the heat, she decided a shower was in order.

Later, when she'd dressed, she felt restless. For once she didn't turn to her painting. Vaguely disturbed without knowing why, she phoned her brother and asked if he'd come over to her place. He told her it would have to be later that night, because he was up at the cabin right then having a look around.

She was surprised and relieved. John was the one person she felt she could talk to about Travis. Her brother might be able to give her insight into how to handle the fact that Travis resented her looking like his deceased wife.

Without a good talk, she feared that when she eventually went to bed, she would lie awake half the night waiting for tomorrow to come. It had been years since she'd found herself wanting to be with a man again. But he wasn't just any man. Since the movie with Casey, she'd thought of his father as her own personal Texas Ranger.

Chapter Five

Travis drove away from the town house and headed downtown. He needed to run by the forensics lab to drop off the soil samples, fingerprint tapes and cast he'd taken.

En route he remembered what he'd wanted to ask Melissa before he'd received that phone call from the school, and everything else had gone out of his mind. He needed a list of any people who'd been in their cabin this year besides family.

Without wasting any time, he phoned her. When she didn't answer, he realized she could be anywhere, doing anything. He left a message for her to call him back.

"Dad? Where are we going?"

"To Lacey and Chaz's condo. They've invited us for dinner."

"Is Zack going to be there?"

"I think so."

"I wish I'd brought Captain America. Can we go home first and get it?"

"Afraid not. We're late as it is."

"But what about Dexter?"

"He'll live till we get back."

When they arrived a few minutes later, everyone noticed that Casey had come without his crutches, and high-fived him.

"Yup," he responded. "Melissa told me my leg was all better and I didn't need them anymore."

"Who's Melissa?" Mitch asked.

"She's my or—" He looked at Travis for help. Everyone in the room cracked up.

"Orthopedic specialist," Travis managed to say without laughing.

"She's awesome and drives a red-and-black Jeep. She used to have a bulldog named Spike, but he's dead now. She made my sore arm all better, too." He extended his scraped elbow for everyone to have a good look.

"Ew!" Zack blurted.

"Does it hurt?" Abby was very worried. Since her bee sting, she was overly solicitous.

"Nope. She put this spray on it."

"She *does* sound awesome," Mitch murmured.

"She is! She gave me a leash for Dexter, and tickets for *Spider-Man*. Dad and I went to the movie with her. Oh, and she bought cupcakes for my whole room. It wasn't really my birthday, but she said it was okay because everyone has a birthday party at school."

Heidi smiled. "That's pretty fantastic."

"Was it a good movie?" Lacey asked him, but her eyes were on Travis.

"Dad thought it was boring, but Melissa and I loved it!"

In the midst of everything Travis's phone rang. He saw the caller ID and said, "Excuse me for a minute."

He left the living room and walked down the hall where he could have some privacy.

"Melissa? Thanks for calling me back."

"Sorry it took me so long. I went to my folks' place for dinner. When I left, I couldn't find my phone. After searching my car, I went back to their house and found it on the couch. It must have slipped right out of my purse."

Her breathless explanation pleased him even more than the knowledge that she hadn't been out with some guy. Travis wasn't blind. She attracted every man in sight. Everywhere they'd been together, he'd seen men's eyes light up the minute they caught sight of her. The traffic in Kamas had slowed several times because some guy was staring at her from his car as they'd walked along the main street.

"No problem. Earlier today I meant to ask you if you would compile a list of people who've been in your cabin this year. I'm talking friends, neighbors, workmen—anyone. Your siblings might be able to help with names, and your parents, too, of course. I'm trying to explore every possibility."

"I'll do it before I go to bed. One more thing, Travis. You'll probably think I'm crazy, but maybe someone is looking for gold and using our cabin to hide at night."

"Gold?"

"I've been thinking about something my grandfather told me when I was young. We were out hiking and he pointed out an old mine that wasn't active anymore. He said that most people thought the gold rush started in California. But he said gold was mined in the western mountains in Utah well before the first white settlers arrived.

"Apparently, Indians first worked the mines here, ones enslaved by the Spanish explorers, who came in the 1600s. In fact, what many originally thought were Indian hieroglyphics and pictographs are actually markers along the Spanish Trail. It led from Mexico to the Uinta Mountains and beyond."

Travis blinked. "I had no idea."

"If he hadn't told me, I wouldn't have known it, either. He said the trail was the main link between Mexico and Spanish outposts here. In the 1800s, pack trains of Mexicans were seen heading out of the Uintas laden with gold.

"Grandpa said all kinds of Spanish cannons and swords were found in our 'killer mountains,' as they called them. One cannon was found in Kamas. They had gold mines that few of the later European arrivals knew about. The ruins of rock homes, forts, tree carvings and various artifacts were clues that pointed the way to the gold ore. Silver, too.

"The Indians knew where the mines were because they'd been forced to work in them by the Spanish. After years of oppression they revolted, killing most of their captors, and returned the gold to the earth, leaving it in the mines. Grandpa told me that from time to time, men have come to Kamas in search of gold, and have checked out that mine right behind our cabin. I know it's a stretch, but since this has been going on most of the summer, it has caused me to wonder."

It *was* a stretch, but he wouldn't dismiss it out of

hand. "Thanks for the Utah history lesson, Melissa. Anything's possible. I'll keep it in mind while I look around."

"Uh-oh. I've got another call coming in, and better hang up. Good night, Travis."

There was a click. He'd wanted to keep on talking. Since that wasn't possible, he turned off his cell phone and returned to the living room. The guys eyed him speculatively, but it was Chaz who asked, "Talking to your latest client?" His friend knew about Melissa's resemblance to Valerie and the shock Travis had received because of it.

Travis nodded. And shouldn't have been surprised when Casey picked up on it immediately. Running over to him, he blurted, "Was it Melissa?" With that question, the guys' wives were looking at him, too.

"As a matter of fact, it was," he admitted.

"I love her! Didn't she want to talk to me?"

Out of the mouths of babes, honest and unabridged. "She had only a minute to answer a question for me," Travis replied.

"Oh."

He didn't know how much of Casey's exclamation had to do with his memory of Valerie, but one thing was certain. His son was hooked on Melissa, and everyone in the room knew it.

"It's time to get you home, bud. Tell Lacey and Chaz thank-you, and thank Heidi and Mitch for the doughnuts."

Casey did so, adding, "It was really yummy. Bye, Zack. Bye, Abby."

Mitch walked over to Travis with a gleam in his eye. "I've yet to hear about all this. Expect a call from me if we don't see each other in the office tomorrow morning."

Travis's friend would be relentless in wanting to find out the details.

Once they arrived home, Casey played with Dexter for a few minutes and took him for a walk on his leash. Finally, it was time for bed. "Come on, bud. Under the covers," Travis said.

As soon as Casey crawled in, the dog jumped up and lay at his feet. Travis kissed his son on the forehead. "Sleep tight. I'll see you in the morning."

"Are you going to take me to the clinic tomorrow to visit Melissa?"

"No. You're fine now."

"But you brought her to school to see me."

"That was different."

"How come?"

He had hoped to avoid the subject, but Casey wouldn't let it go. Since Travis didn't know how long this case for Melissa's family might go on, he realized he needed to tell his son a few facts.

With a resigned sigh, he sank onto the side of his bed. "The reason she was with me today was because I've been hired by her father to do some investigative work. I understand you told Melissa I'm a P.I."

"Yup. At the movie."

"Well, she told her dad. He asked me to look around their mountain cabin up in Kamas and find out who's been living in it without their permission."

Casey gasped. "You mean someone has been sneaking inside?"

"It looks like it. I took Melissa with me today so she could show me where it is and let me in."

"Is it far away?" His son's voice had a mournful note.

"No. Only forty-five minutes. It's up by Park City. Do you remember we went up there skiing?"

"Yes." But Casey looked unhappy.

"Melissa and I were on the way down the canyon when someone from your school called me."

"Is her cabin big?"

"Sort of. It has an upstairs and is made of logs because it's old."

"Cool. Can I see it sometime with you and Melissa?"

"I think it's a possibility." After fighting his conflicted feelings for Melissa from day one, Travis was surprised he'd conceded that much to Casey. Something was happening to him. Today, with Melissa, he'd had moments he wished could have gone on.

"Are you going to go up with her tomorrow?"

"Probably." She wanted to paint. Travis couldn't very well tell her she couldn't come, but the scenario was starting to get complicated in ways he didn't feel like examining.

"Why can't I go with you?"

"You know why. You have school."

"No, I don't. Tomorrow is teachers' work day."

Travis blinked. He'd forgotten about that.

"I don't want to go to Aunt Pat's. I want to be with you. What if you don't come back?"

Travis knew that deep-seated fear was always lurking beneath the surface. He pulled his son into his arms. "Tell you what. I'll phone her. Maybe we can all go up for part of the day. How does that sound?"

"Hooray!" In an instant, his boy became a happy child again. They high-fived. "I can't wait till tomorrow. Night, Daddy."

Travis discovered he couldn't wait, either, and reached for his phone to call Melissa for a second time. Hopefully, whatever she was doing, she'd pick up.

She answered on the third ring.

He liked her well-modulated voice. "Hi. I know it's getting late, but there's one more thing I wanted to talk to you about before you're in bed. Are you free to talk?"

There was a pause, then she said, "Is there a new development in the case?"

He frowned when she answered his question with a question. Something was definitely off. She wasn't the same warm woman from earlier, and she didn't mention Casey in the conversation, which wasn't like her. "I can tell you're not alone."

"My brother's here, helping me with that list. He just got down from the cabin."

Travis's blood turned cold. "Did he go alone?"

"Yes." She paused for a second. "Are you saying it wasn't a good idea? I thought it would be okay for him. He wanted to look around."

"After today I'm concerned, because I suspect that more than one person has been using your place to sleep. I don't like the implications, and feel it won't be safe for you or anyone in your family to go up there unless I'm with you."

He heard her quiet gasp. "You're not telling me everything you know, are you?"

"I'm operating on instinct right now, Melissa." He grimaced. "It's too soon to give you facts. What's important is that you and your family will come to no harm if you stay strictly away. If it's necessary for one of you to go up, and I can't be there, then I'll send some of my backup crew to protect you. Be sure you tell your brother how serious this is. I'm sorry it has to be this way."

"So am I. But if you say it's dangerous, I believe you. John's totally impressed with all your surveillance gadgets. He's fascinated by the work you do and can't wait to meet you."

"I look forward to meeting him. In the meantime, all is not lost. Casey's school is taking a teacher work day tomorrow, so he'll be free. We'll pick you up around ten and drive to the cabin. While I'm busy checking around the area, you can paint to your heart's content, as long as you and Casey stay within fifty feet of the cabin. Two of my crew will already be around to keep everyone safe."

"You mean it?" The excitement was back in her voice—the sound that had been missing. The one he'd wanted to hear. "You don't know how I long to take advantage of this weather. I love the mountains this time of year."

"I'm aware you took a week off from work to paint, Melissa. Even though your father hired me, and I need to be up there to do the job he's paying me to do, there's nothing to prevent you from being with me. Under the circumstances it will be best if we take your Jeep, so anyone keeping a lookout will know you're in residence and won't come around while we're there."

"No problem. Casey told me he wanted to ride in it."

"Now he's going to get his chance. On the way up the canyon we'll pick up pizza to take with us. There's a place in the Bell Canyon Plaza."

"I know the one."

"Since Casey learned you have a cabin, he's dying to see it. Is it all right if we bring Dexter?"

"Oh, yes!" Clearly, she adored animals. "He'll love it up there. I want to draw him. Terriers are so darling."

Melissa had Travis smiling. "Then it's settled. See you tomorrow." He hung up, excited to know he'd be with her soon. He was also pleased at the idea of taking their Scottie along. Besides being fun for Casey, Dexter made an excellent watchdog.

Too wired to go to bed yet, Travis went to his study. He needed to write up notes on the case and email them to Roman, to keep him abreast of his progress. Travis had no idea what he'd find up there tomorrow, but he planned to hike around and look for signs of people camping in an undesignated area.

Melissa's suggestion that people might be up there trying to find a lost gold mine might not be so far-fetched. She was a regular treasure trove of information. It was one more facet of her personality that drew him.

Next, he phoned Jose and asked him to drive up to Grampy's in the morning. Travis wanted photos of the employees who showed up for work. He gave Jose a description of the man who'd leered at Melissa.

"If he drives a car to work, I want you to get his license plate number. But whether in a car or on foot, follow him after he gets off work. I'd like to know what he does in his spare time. Find out if he has friends in the area. See if he lives alone or with someone."

The man might not have anything to do with the case, but Travis was curious about him and intended to check him out. Oftentimes evidence turned up that was helpful for an entirely different case the police were investigating.

"I'd also like you to find out who's the new owner of Grampy's. Melissa said the place changed hands in July."

"Okay. Anything else?"

"Will you check the water and electricity bills for their cabin? Let's monitor the usage and compare this last month's activity to the bills for last year. I'm looking for any disparities or an unexpected spike."

"I'll get on it first thing tomorrow."

After they got off the phone he contacted Adam and asked him to set up surveillance while he was up there with his son and Melissa tomorrow.

Finally, Travis had done everything he could for the moment, and left the study. A shower sounded good. He headed for the bathroom, full of anticipation for tomorrow.

He could see why Melissa loved the cabin so much. Salt Lake was unique. Within a half hour you could be in a remote mountain wilderness, thousands of feet above the valley floor. He'd hated leaving the Davis Mountains in Texas, which he loved, but today's outing with Melissa, in a more primitive setting, where the peaks knifed the rarified air, called to the deepest part of him.

And when they'd been up in the rustic bedroom she'd turned into a studio, their eyes had met across the room. For a moment he'd imagined the cabin being theirs. Everything appealed to him, from the artwork on the walls to the colorful quilt her grandmother had made years earlier. Mellow with age and life having been lived, the cabin's interior had a warmth he could feel. Casey would love it. Especially the rope swing.

He saw black when he thought of the intruders who'd ruined Melissa's pleasure. Travis now had another enemy he was tracking besides Valerie's killer. This new project had become personal.

THE MINUTE MELISSA EMERGED from her town house on Tuesday morning, Casey came running, with an adorable black Scottish terrier at his heels.

"Hi, Casey!" she called out, and was rewarded with a hearty hug around the waist. "This must be Dexter. Hiya, fella." She hunkered down to rub his head and ears.

After lots of licks from his pink tongue, she got up and unlocked the Jeep. Travis picked up the dog and put him in the backseat with Casey.

"Quite a change from the first time we showed up at the clinic," he whispered as he came around to shut her door.

Their eyes met. "But he *did* look so cute using his crutches," she whispered back.

"Are you talking about me?"

She turned to peer at the dark-haired boy, strapped in with the dog lying next to him.

"Yes. We're glad your leg is all better. Let me see your arm." He showed it to her. "You're going to have a scab, but it's healing just fine."

"Since you sprayed me, it doesn't hurt anymore."

His father grinned at Melissa, turning her limbs to water.

She'd confided in John about Travis's deceased wife and her own resemblance to her. John didn't have specific answers to that problem, but had warned Melissa to go slowly. In time, things would change with Travis one way or the other. Her brother advised her to just play it cool while the investigation was going on.

Hah. So much for trying to distance herself from Travis. This talk with John had come too late. She was already in up to her hairline where the Texas Ranger was concerned. Any more looks like he'd just given her and she'd drown.

Melissa started the engine and they took off. "I'm glad you're so much better," she said to Casey. "I was thinking maybe you'd like to do some painting with me. Around the side of the cabin is a big rock where a family of woodchucks play. They have five burrows I've counted. Sometimes they stand still on their hind legs, listening for intruders, and then they whistle to warn the others."

Casey laughed. "They whistle?"

"Yes. Some people call them pig-whistlers. My brother calls them pot guts, because they have such big tummies." Both father and son laughed this time. "I think they're fun to draw," Melissa added.

"I wanna see them."

"You will, but we'll have to sit quietly for a while until they come out."

"I can be quiet, huh, Dad?"

"When you're asleep," his father teased. "But I can't vouch for Dexter."

"I'll keep him in the cabin. Will that be okay, Melissa?"

"Of course." She pulled up to the pizza place in the plaza. "I've got some old doggie toys of Spike's I couldn't bring myself to throw away." Travis sent her a compassionate glance. "Dexter can play with those while we're out watching for the woodchucks. Then we'll let him come outside so he can have fun."

Casey beamed while Travis went inside to pick up their lunch. After he came back, the smell of pizza filled the car while she drove them up the canyon. By the time they reached the cabin, everyone was starving, so they decided to eat before doing anything else.

When Travis announced he was off to do some hiking, Casey seemed fine with it. So was Melissa, because she knew some of Travis's men were outside, guarding them. But though she pretended nothing affected her, underneath, she worried about him. He'd said it was too dangerous for her to be up here without him and his crew, but who would protect Travis?

After asking herself that question, she realized how important he'd become to her. So important he was all she thought about. She'd had a life before he came into it, but she couldn't remember what it was like.

Melissa knew he enjoyed her company, but he'd done nothing overt to act on any feelings he might have for her. As she'd told John, if Travis still saw his wife when he was with her, you wouldn't know it. Her brother had suggested it was possible Travis was holding back because he was doing a job for her family, and didn't mix his private life with his professional one.

Melissa didn't have answers yet, but something needed to change soon. She couldn't bear to be with him like this, not knowing what was going on inside him. Maybe *nothing* was going on, and she was fantasizing at her own peril. That thought just about killed her.

Travis didn't return until it was getting dark and time to go home. She'd fixed peanut butter sandwiches. Luckily, it was food Casey liked. When his dad walked in, Casey asked if they could sleep over, but his father nixed that idea so fast it surprised even Melissa. Since his return she'd sensed his preoccupation.

In the car on the way down, Casey made up for his father's silence by telling him about the squirrels that had come out to play instead of the pig-whistlers. While he regaled Travis with their activities, Dexter chewed on one of the toys he'd commandeered.

They looked like a happy family coming home from a trip to the mountains, but the picture was false. Melissa's stomach was in knots by the time she drove them back to her town house.

They all got out of the Jeep, and Casey said, "I wish I didn't have school tomorrow."

"But you do," Travis said, without his usual warmth.

Melissa bit her lip. "Good night, Casey. Thanks for bringing Dexter."

"He loved it. We had fun!"

"So did I."

"See ya!"

"Good night, Melissa." Travis's low voice worked its way beneath her skin, igniting every nerve ending. She felt as if he'd brought her out of a deep sleep. Now she didn't know where to go with all these awakened feelings.

Travis bundled his son and dog into his truck before she could say good-night back. When she reached the door of her condo, he waved to her before she let herself inside.

Too uptight to relax, she got busy doing laundry, then talked with her mom for a few minutes before taking a shower. When Melissa was finally ready for bed, she still couldn't settle down.

After wrapping a robe around herself, she went into the living room to watch the ten o'clock news, hoping it would help her get sleepy. She'd just pressed the remote when her cell phone rang. Her heart thudded as she reached for it. When she saw who was calling, she could hardly breathe.

"Travis."

"Sorry for calling you this late."

"It's all right." *More than all right.* "I'm still up."

"I got a call from work while I was out hiking earlier. Something's come up that requires me to be in the office tomorrow. But the guys are keeping you under constant surveillance, so you can go up whenever you want."

"That's great. Thank you." Except the idea of being at the cabin without him suddenly didn't seem as appealing. Their two sojourns up there had spoiled her. It wasn't just a matter of him making her feel safe. She'd come to enjoy his company. Really enjoy it. "Do you think you'll be able to get away from the office at some point?" *You're pushing it, Melissa.*

"I'm counting on it. After school I'll pick up Casey and bring him to the cabin with Dexter." The news gave her heart a workout. "I'm afraid my son worries about me leaving him when I have business away from Salt Lake. He's still afraid that I might never come back."

"That doesn't surprise me at all." Her voice caught. Losing Travis was too tragic to contemplate. Casey needed him terribly. "Tell you what. If you're going to do that, I'll fix dinner up there," she said without hesitation. "I promise I can do better than peanut butter sandwiches." She'd been afraid she might not be seeing him tomorrow, and now was ecstatic. "What else does Casey like besides pizza?"

"Candy and doughnuts."

Melissa's laughter was like sunshine.

"Hot dogs are a safe bet," Travis told her. "He's not a big eater."

"And what about his dad? Would he like steak fajitas?"

Travis lounged against the wall, enjoying their conversation more than a little. "I've heard he's rather partial to them."

"Then I'll inform the cook. If I know her, she'll make a surprise dessert guaranteed to satisfy your boy's sweet tooth."

"Tell the cook he gets that particular tooth from me."

She chuckled quietly. "Thanks for the tip. Give me a ring when you reach the church parking lot in Kamas and I'll drive down to get you."

"We'll be watching for you. Good night, Melissa."

"Good night."

No sooner had Travis turned off his bedroom light to go to sleep than his cell phone rang. It was quarter to eleven. His excitement that it might be Melissa with something else she wanted to tell him subsided when he reached for it and saw the caller ID. Jose. He must have something important or he would have waited till morning to phone.

"Jose? What's up?"

"I'm still in Kamas. The guy got off work at eight. I followed him to a cabin in the forest about a mile west of town. It was shuttered and looked locked up for the season. There was a garage next to it, and he went inside there."

"Give me the coordinates and I'll check to find out the name of the owner." It was possible Melissa would know. After jotting down the information, Travis said, "Then what happened?"

"After a while he and another guy came out. It was too dark for details, but the second guy was smaller. More wiry. They locked the garage door and took off into the forest with a flashlight. I figured I had time to look around, and undid the lock. Inside was a 2005 Fleetwood Tioga 25' Class C RV camper, but it was locked."

"Something's definitely going on."

"Agreed. It had a Utah plate and up-to-date registration. I walked back to my truck before phoning it in. They'll call me when they know anything. What do you want me to do next?"

"Ask Lon to coordinate with you and Adam. I want to know where that camper goes when it leaves the garage."

"Will do."

"Thanks, Jose."

Travis hung up, gratified that his suspicions hadn't proved wrong, even if the situation might not have anything to do with the Roberts case. He stretched out in bed, reliving the day with Melissa. So far he'd seen her only with her hair done in different styles away from her face. He wondered what that light ash-brown hair would look like loose and flowing. How it would feel to bury his face in it…

When Casey woke him up the next morning, the last thing Travis remembered thinking was that Melissa had been on his mind, not Valerie. That was a first.

Now that he thought about it, he recalled that Chaz had experienced something similar. His friend had lost his first wife to cancer before he'd done his stint with the Navy SEALs. Not until last spring had he become emotionally involved with another woman. One night he'd confided to Travis that he knew Lacey was the one when he'd found himself dreaming about her, instead of his deceased wife. It had happened the first night he'd met Lacey, during his investigation of her stalking case.

Travis wasn't thinking Melissa was "the one," far from it. He wasn't in the market for another wife. But he had to admit no other woman since Valerie had interested him to this extent. The problem was, he didn't trust this attraction. Was it because, deep down, he wanted a woman who reminded him of Valerie? Maybe. How sick was that?

Casey followed him out of the bathroom, where Travis had just finished shaving. "Can Melissa come to dinner at our house tonight?"

Travis wasn't surprised that that was the first question to pop out of his son's mouth. He could hardly avoid this situation while he was working her case. Once he'd pulled on jeans and another T-shirt, he turned to his son. "Guess what? I'm going to pick you up after school and we're driving to the cabin again. Melissa's fixing dinner for us."

"Hooray!" Casey ran to the kitchen, whooping the whole way. Travis followed, to fix them fruit and cereal. Once they'd fed Dexter, they left for school in the truck.

After dropping off Casey with a hug, Travis stopped for gas, then headed to the office. Jose and Roman were waiting for him with coffee and doughnuts. The boss had a big smile on his face. "Come on in."

Bemused, Travis reached for his coffee and sat down, eyeing both of them. "What's going on?"

"Congratulations are in order."

Chapter Six

"What are you talking about?"

Roman smiled. "I'll let Jose tell you."

Travis eyed the other man. "Is this about that camper?"

His colleague nodded. "An hour after I phoned in the license plate number, I got a call. That Utah plate was stolen off a new blue Jetta on June 5 of this year. So they checked to see if the camper was stolen."

"Wait till you hear this next part," Roman interjected.

Travis was all ears.

"The police in Cochise County, Arizona, have been looking for the killer of an elderly couple, a crime that happened on June 3 of this year. They were found in their home in Douglas, with their camper stolen. I checked the VIN number, and it's their camper, all right. As you know, Douglas is in that border territory between the U.S. and Mexico."

Travis's heart dropped any time he heard that another innocent person had been murdered. It hit too close to home. But a part of him was elated that his hunch had been on target.

"What about the man you followed?"

"Adam said the guy came back to the garage about an hour later and got in the camper. He was in there all night, and still is. He thinks the guy's living there. The other man disappeared into the woods and never came back."

Travis's mind was reeling with possibilities. "This could be connected to what's going on at the Roberts cabin. Considering the close proximity between the camper and their place, that other man could be making himself at home there. But it's still early days."

"I agree," Roman said.

Travis looked at his boss. "Let's sit on what we know for now, and just keep them under surveillance. I'll be talking to forensics in a few minutes, to see what they've come up with so far. Later on I'll be going up to the cabin again, to check the tapes and the listening device.

"Before we make official inquiries, I'll ask Melissa if she knows who owns that vacant cabin and garage. I meant to ask her earlier, but got distracted. If the intruders were there last night, then we'll know a lot more than we do now, and can decide how to proceed. Jose? Have we found out who bought Grampy's yet?"

"Lon's still working on it. Hopefully he'll get back to us sometime today."

Roman leaned forward. "You're on to something big, Travis. I feel it in my bones." His solemn expression changed to a gleeful one. "I barely put you on the case and already you've turned up a couple of possible killers."

Travis eyed Jose. "Thanks to a great backup team."

"Agreed," Roman said. "How did you know about the hidden camper?"

"On Monday the guy with the buzz cut waited on Melissa and me at Grampy's, this burger shop in Kamas. He leered at her in a way that alarmed her. I sensed something about him wasn't right, so I asked Jose to check him out."

Their boss grinned. "And just like that you've helped solve cases that have stumped lawmen in two states. I'll get the police chief on the phone. He'll contact the cops in Douglas, but I'll make it clear you're in the middle of a sting and don't want anything to leak until you find out what's going on at the cabin."

"Appreciate that, Roman."

"You were born with an instinct for this business, comrade. Talk to you later."

Travis nodded and stood up. "Come to my office, Jose. Let's listen to what Forensics has to say."

A few minutes later Travis had Rudy, in Forensics, on the line. He was the best in the business. "What have you got for us?" Travis turned on the speakerphone so Jose could hear.

"That tire print was pretty good. I saw two cuts that could have been made by rocks or glass. They're year-old Goodyear tires.

"As for the fingerprints, you got some decent ones off that pine table you noted on the tape. I've sent them on to headquarters, and they'll run them through the database. The other items had some interesting elements."

"Like what?" Travis hadn't realized he was holding his breath.

"For example, the soil sample contained traces of mashed foliage typical of that area of forest. It also contained marijuana."

"Marijuana?" Travis's eyebrows lifted as he stared at Jose in amazement.

"No doubt it was clinging to the soles of someone's shoes. The particular type is called Early Misty. It's a short, bushy plant that flowers in eight weeks. The sample was pretty fresh. So were the cigarette butts you brought in last evening. They matched the others that were days old, and in some instances, a couple of months old."

"Were you able to identify the brand?"

"Yes. That's interesting, too. The tobacco is a type grown in Japan and shipped to Europe, where it's made into cigarettes with the brand name Monte Carlo. These are the long, slim kind you find in cellophane bundles."

"I've heard of them. Thanks, Rudy. Couldn't do this without you." Travis clicked off. "Jose? What do you know about Monte Carlo cigarettes?"

"They're the strong-flavored variety and the cheapest on the world market. You can buy them online in the U.S., but they're distributed and sold in Switzerland, Germany, Monaco, the Emirates and Colombia."

"We're narrowing it down. These boys have to be illegals sent by some Colombian drug cartel to work here."

Jose nodded. "The traffickers come primarily from the Valle del Cauca region or from the Caribbean north coast. The latter operate more independently than the Cali mafia, but are very powerful. By working with counterparts in Mexico and the U.S., they're responsible for most of the world's cocaine production and wholesale distribution."

Travis leaned back in his chair. "I wasn't in Utah three years ago, but I remember hearing Roman talk about a crop of marijuana plants with a street value of $60 million found growing on a mountain farther south in this state."

"You're talking Boulder Mountain in Wayne County. It was headed by a Mexican cartel."

"Could be the Colombians have done the same thing around here in the back country. The man you saw come out of the garage could be one of that group. Then again, maybe there's no connection."

"Maybe not," Jose murmured, "but I'm planning to get a look at the left front tire on that camper, in case it made a trip to the cabin. That will give us the link you're trying to find."

"Good. While you do that, I'll be busy hiking in the mountains, looking for marijuana plants."

As Jose got up to leave, Travis called him back. "I have another question for you. While Melissa and I were getting our hamburgers, I noticed the guy with the buzz had a tattoo on the back of his neck." Travis's eyes narrowed. "Does a solid silver star with eight points mean anything to you?"

Jose looked astonished, then shook his head in disbelief.

Travis half laughed. "What?"

"You just solved another piece of the puzzle. That star is in the middle of the Barranquilla flag, the northern port city of Colombia. It was carried by Simon Bolivar, signifying the eight provinces of the confederacy."

Again Travis's mind was off and running. "The bunch of them could have come up through the Caribbean to Mexico. When they got across the Arizona border, they killed that couple for the camper and drove straight here."

"It's more than a possibility."

"We don't know how many illegals are involved in this operation, but it's been well orchestrated up to now," Travis theorized. "Otherwise, they wouldn't have found a garage to keep the stolen vehicle hidden two days after that couple was killed. Roman needs to hear about this new development."

"While you talk to him, I'll drive back up to Kamas and try to get a look at those camper tires. When I find something out, I'll phone you. Oh, one more thing. I checked the bills with the water and electric company for this year and last. There was no abnormal usage of either utility."

"These men are being careful. It's more evidence that this operation has been in the planning for a long time."

"Watch your back, Travis."

"Ditto."

After Jose left, Travis went back to their boss's office and gave him the latest update. The news about the marijuana blew Roman away. They talked strategy before Travis went back to his office and called his resource at the database down at police headquarters. He wanted to know if any of those fingerprints were a match for wanted felons operating illegally in the country. The Feds would have a field day.

Later, Mitch dropped into his office, and they decided to go to lunch. Travis told him about Melissa, and they talked shop. Before long it was time to pick up Casey. His son worried when Travis didn't get to school right on time, but his anxiety level hadn't been as high since he'd met Melissa.

Casey was crazy about her. There were moments when he seemed to be as happy around her as he'd been when his mom was alive. And he wasn't the only one....

Time had something to do with the healing process, but Travis had to admit Melissa was playing a big part. Otherwise he wouldn't find himself this eager to be with her again. For several days he'd been wondering what she would taste like. Before much more time went on, he would have to find out—or go mad with wanting.

MELISSA REVELED IN BEING able to paint for a whole day without fear. At three o'clock she put her things away and started dinner. Around four she drove down to the church parking lot to wait for Travis and Casey. Her heart thudded when she heard the phone ring. She clicked on and said hello.

"Melissa?"

"Casey, hi! Where are you?"

"Dad says we're just coming into Kamas."

"Well, I'm right here watching for you."

"Okay. Don't go away."

She laughed. "I promise I won't."

A few minutes later they pulled in alongside her, and

everyone, including Dexter, got into her Jeep. The hug Casey gave her was so natural, she was thrilled to the core. It was sheer delight to hear about his school day. She caught Travis's warm glance. No ice, no shadows today. Her spirits soared.

Once they reached the cabin, Travis disappeared outside, while Casey ran around examining everything. After he'd teased Dexter with more of Spike's toys, he became Melissa's shadow.

She set up an easel for him and they painted out on the front porch. He chatted about some of the kids in his class at school. Robbie had asthma and had to carry around a spray. Cindy's daddy had to move to California because her parents got a divorce. Melissa loved listening to it all, but when she heard Casey's tummy growl, so loudly they both laughed and Dexter barked, she knew it was time for dinner.

Travis came in as she was putting supper on the table. To Melissa it felt like they were a real family. She found it harder and harder not to fantasize about what was going on. While he washed his hands at the kitchen sink, her gaze took in his rock-hard physique. The play of muscle across his back and shoulders kept her attention riveted.

When he suddenly turned toward the table, he caught her staring at him, and she felt herself blush to her eyebrows. Casey saved the moment. "Come on, Dad. We're hungry."

"So am I."

After they'd tucked into their food, Travis glanced at her. "I did some hiking and made the rounds of the cabins in the area you identified for me. There was one with a detached garage near the main road, about a mile from town, but it was boarded up. Do you have any idea who it belongs to?"

"You must mean the Gledhills. They're a retired couple from Reno, Nevada. They were willed that cabin by her father, but only come up here every other year. On the off year they like to boat on Lake Tahoe."

"That explains it," Travis murmured. "This afternoon I was able to talk to most of the people in the other cabins. When I showed them my ID, they were very receptive and anxious to talk to me. However, their complaints had more to do with thefts of fishing gear and items of furniture taken mostly over the winter months.

"I found it interesting that so far none of them have complained of intruders living there when the owners aren't about. Yet that seems to be the particular problem of *your* cabin. My hunch is because it's the highest one on this side of the ridge, out of sight."

"I'm sure that's true. The very thing I love about this location is what makes it a natural target for evi— for bad people," she corrected. Casey picked up on everything.

His father's eyes went an intense dark blue. "They won't be doing it much longer. That's a promise." The almost primitive note in his voice convinced her he knew more than he'd told her. The Texas Ranger was on the hunt. Melissa's hand trembled as she reached for her water glass.

"If you two will excuse me," Travis said next, "I have some work to do upstairs."

"Go ahead, Dad. We'll make dessert."

Travis exchanged an amused glance with Melissa, then left the table.

"Okay, Casey, let's get busy." She brought a dish from the counter. "These chocolate chips are melted. I'll let you ice the brownies."

She scooped the chocolate onto the cold peppermint butter cream frosting, then handed him the spoon. "While the chocolate is hot, you spread it around lightly and quickly till the brownies are all covered. Try not to mix the two together too much, so it will stay layered."

"Like this?" He made big fast swirls.

"That's perfect."

He worked with concentration, biting his lower lip. "I've finished! Now can I lick the spoon and the pot?"

Melissa chuckled before setting the brownies aside. While he went to town on the leftover chocolate, she cut a big brownie for Travis and put it on a plate. With a napkin in hand, she walked upstairs and found him in the hall, putting more film in the video camera. Melissa couldn't help watching him.

His jeans molded to his long, powerful legs. Her gaze traveled to a well-defined chest covered in a coffee-colored polo. In the dim light coming from downstairs, half of his chiseled features and rich chestnut hair were hidden in shadow. No superlative would do him justice. She only knew that when she looked at him, her senses came alive.

"Do you need my help?" she asked.

"I'm all through here, thanks." He put the camera back in place at the top of the stairs.

She moved closer. "Here's a treat for your efforts."

When Travis turned to her, his eyes swept over her before he took the brownie and bit into it. After swallowing, he said, "You have to be kidding."

"What do you mean?"

"I thought you told me you needed a cook. This brownie is too good to be true." He ate the rest in one swallow. "You could make your living selling these. Move over, Bauer Doughnuts. Dalton Brownies is the new company in town."

"Travis…" Warmth spread through her like the chocolate Casey was licking in the kitchen.

"It's true. The fajitas were wonderful, too. I don't think there's anything you can't do. I thought the same that first morning in your office. Like magic, you got Casey to give up his crutches long enough to walk around the room with you. You're like the Pied Piper of Hamelin."

Outwardly, Melissa smiled, but inside she was sad because there was one thing she couldn't do. She couldn't change her appearance. The reminder of his wife would always be there whenever he looked at her. "Thanks for the compliment, but I'll let you in on a secret. You don't realize it yet, but you've seen my whole repertoire."

"I don't think so." He smiled. "Every time we're together you do something that surprises me and delights my son."

"*He* delights *me*. I believe he'd make a great Texas Ranger. He notices everything. I know about every kid in his class—whose parents are getting divorced, whose grandma has cancer, whose daddy bashed in his mother's car when he drove into the garage, who keeps snakes in their basement."

Travis's shoulders shook with laughter.

"He reminds me of someone else I've recently met," she teased. "And you're right. He does have your sweet tooth."

"You just said the magic word," Travis murmured. "Let's go downstairs. It's so quiet down there, I need to check on him. But the real reason is because I have to have more of these brownies." What would it be like if he ever kissed her and told her he had to have more kisses?

When they entered the kitchen, Casey looked up. "Hi, Dad!" The smile on his handsome little face was wreathed in chocolate.

Travis crossed to him. "It looks like you licked the platter clean."

"Huh? This is a *pot*."

Travis shot Melissa an amused glance. The old Mother Goose rhyme was wasted on his son, but she got the message and smiled. When he smiled back, she felt like she was floating.

To hide her reaction, she wet a paper towel for Casey to use to wipe off his mouth. Travis stood at the table and downed two more brownies in quick succession.

"Can I have a brownie now, Dad?"

"A little one. You've got enough chocolate in you to keep you awake for a week."

"Huh?"

"Your dad doesn't want you to get a stomachache,"

Melissa interjected. "I'll wrap up the rest of the brownies so you can take them home."

"Thanks! Can we play Go Fish now?" She'd found a deck of cards in the game closet.

"One round," his father decreed. "After that we've got to get you home to bed."

Melissa cleaned up the rest of the dishes, then joined them. Casey made the most matches, and was proclaimed the winner in no time, before they turned out the lights and locked up. This evening had filled her with such contentment, it was scary.

She put Casey in charge of the brownies as they walked out to the Jeep. While she drove, he sat in the back and chattered all the way down to the truck parked in town. When she pulled up next to it, Travis got out and put his son in the backseat. She hated it that their marvelous evening was over.

After buckling him in, Travis came around to her side of the Jeep. She lowered the window. Their faces were only inches apart. It was madness, but she ached for him to kiss her. If he ever got the urge, would he pretend she was his wife? She couldn't bear it if that were true.

His eyes played over her features. "You made this evening more memorable for us than you know." She felt his warm breath on her face. Only a little closer... "How do I thank you?"

The blood pounded in her ears. "You're already doing that by agreeing to track down the trespassers."

He let out a sigh. She thought maybe he didn't like remembering he had a job to do. At least for a little while.

"Speaking of your case, I was wondering if tomorrow you'd come hiking in the forest beyond the ridge with me. This evening didn't give me nearly enough time to do all the necessary exploring. I'm aware you want to paint, but you grew up here and know the area better than most people."

Melissa needed to remember the man wasn't asking her out. He needed her help. Since she'd been the one to tell her father about Lufka's, and spearhead this investigation in the first place, she wanted to do whatever she could for it to be solved.

"Finding the culprits is more important than my painting. Besides, I got in a full day today. I told you I'd help all I can, and I meant it. What time do you want to leave in the morning?"

"I'll be by at eight-thirty, after I've dropped Casey off at school. In case you didn't notice, he's had a wonderful time with you today. Thank you for taking the time to paint with him and play games." Travis's eyes held a faraway look just then. "He's been missing that."

Travis had been missing it, too, Melissa knew. She had a hard time swallowing. "The feeling's mutual. Your son is precious. Do you want me to drive my Jeep tomorrow? If so, I'll need to fill it with gas when I get down the canyon tonight."

"Since we're going to a new area, I thought we'd take my truck. It shouldn't be too much longer before I get a lead. Bring a backpack with the things you'll want."

What Melissa wanted was right here, and she didn't want to have to wait until tomorrow. "I'll be ready."

It was all she could do to start down the canyon

without breaking into tears for the no-win situation in which she found herself.

Yes, she knew Travis was grateful for her help. The three of them got along well and they had a lot of fun, but she'd been playing house the whole time. When he caught the people invading the cabin, it would all be over, and she'd be headed for heartache.

He followed her all the way to her town house, but that came as no surprise. Travis had had sound instincts to guard and protect. After Russ, she was lucky to meet a man like Travis and get to know him. He was living proof that some men were a breed apart. Valerie had been blessed to know his love.

Melissa took a deep breath as she parked her car and got out. She noticed Travis was still out in front. He hadn't pulled away yet. "You don't need to watch while I go inside," she called to him.

"I beg to differ. If I'd gone to the store with Valerie, she might still be alive."

With that revealing response, joy went out of Melissa's world. But it was the wake-up call she'd needed to get out of her dream state.

Tonight's activities had brought back happier memories for him from the past, but it couldn't be clearer that he would always miss his wife. Up until now Melissa had assumed her resemblance to Valerie had worked against her. But after what he'd just said, she decided he wasn't interested in any woman. He had a son to raise. That was enough for him.

Heartsick, she resolved to keep the situation between

them strictly business. It might be the end of her, but that was the way it had to be.

"See ya!" Casey shouted.

She waved to him from her front door. It was a good thing neither of them could see the tears in her eyes. "See ya," she said softly.

Chapter Seven

"Bye, Dexter," Casey said. "You've got plenty of food and water. I left you a doggie treat."

Travis glanced over his shoulder. They'd just finished breakfast and were ready to leave the house. He put some bottled water in his backpack for the hike. "Casey? What are you doing now?"

"I'm cutting some brownies to take for my school snack." He got out the foil and wrapped them up before putting them in his backpack.

Travis couldn't help laughing because he'd had the same idea. He went over to the counter and cut two brownies for himself, which he proceeded to eat on their way out to the truck.

"I think Melissa's food is as good as Mom's."

Whoa. Travis hadn't been prepared for that, but it was clear his son had moved on. "Yeah, these brownies are the best I've ever tasted."

"Yup. She makes good hot dogs, too. Can she come over tonight?"

"We'll see."

"You always say that."

Travis glanced at him. "What would you like me to say?"

Casey looked at him with innocent eyes. "Just say yes."

Travis chuckled at his son's remark. It was so...adult. He was still chuckling when he dropped Casey off at school and then pulled up in front of Melissa's town house five minutes later. She came hurrying out to the truck before he'd even opened his door. He got out and put her backpack in the rear seat with his.

"What's so funny?" she asked.

When he told her, she chuckled, too. "He's an original if ever there was one."

"So," Travis said, "after our hike, do you want to make his day and come to our house for dinner? I'll order Chinese."

She didn't hesitate. "Only if I can bring something to contribute."

"I think Casey's hoping you'll make more brownies. Me, too."

She rolled her eyes. "More?"

"There was only one left when we walked out the door this morning. It'll be a race to see who gets it when Casey and I return to the house later."

"If that's what you really want."

"It is. Believe me."

Her fragrance, whether from the shower or her shampoo, met his nostrils. He was becoming addicted to it. "I do believe you're the most punctual woman I ever met."

As she climbed into the cab, the action revealed the lush curves of her body. She'd come dressed in denims and a long-sleeved crew-neck in an oatmeal color. He helped her in and shut the door before going around.

After they were on the road she flashed him a guile-less smile. "My brother says that a girl being on time makes a guy nervous. He says it's one of my most ir-ritating qualities."

Travis chuckled. "If he's rarely on time, then you make him feel guilty. In my business punctuality is an absolute necessity."

"Oh, good," she said drily. "Now I feel much better."

"I was paying you a compliment."

Melissa laughed. "I know. Thank you. What's the plan for today?"

"I'm going to let you decide where we go. We'll hike beyond the ridge and look in the high back country for people who might be up to no good. It'll be better if we don't talk while we're moving. When we stop, we'll whisper."

"Okay."

He pulled a Geological Survey map out of the glove compartment and handed it to her. "This is one I took from the cabin drawer. Let me know how much of the terrain you're familiar with. I'll drive us up to one of the firebreak roads. When we find a good spot, we'll pull off and walk from there."

She opened the map. He glanced at her as she stud-ied it. Her lovely profile was beguiling, and with her hair caught back in a tortoiseshell clip, sheerly elegant. For once he wished he was on vacation and they could enjoy the day doing whatever they wanted. From the first she'd gotten to him, thrilling him at odd moments.

Now those moments were merging. When he was away from her, he thought about her more and more....

Yet part of him still felt an illogical resentment for those thoughts. He and Casey had been surviving in a numb state until that first day at the clinic. When she'd greeted them at the door, it was as if Travis had walked out of a black-and-white movie into a world of blinding Technicolor. Besides conjuring up remembered pain from the past, new feelings burgeoned. Longings and yearnings had taken hold, surprising the hell out of him.

He understood the initial attraction because of her similarities to Valerie. But to go on seeing Melissa as anyone but a client, desiring her to the point that he ached to act on his feelings, thrust him into an unexpected realm of guilt. Valerie hadn't been gone that long. It seemed a desecration of her memory that he wanted this woman sitting next to him. But he couldn't stop what his body was telling him.

Outside Kamas, Travis took a right and drove up an emergency access road into the forest. When he found a natural turnout, he pulled into it and parked. "What do you think?" He leaned over to look at the map. Her warm cheek was too close to his, distracting him from the business at hand. He'd become acutely aware of her.

If she was disturbed by his closeness, she hid it well. "I've hiked all through the forest this side of the ridge. But I hiked on the other side only once, with my grandpa. That's the area with the mine. The slope is steeper there, and the forest is thick, making it difficult to walk."

"Okay then," he said, "we'll hike in the area you're

most familiar with and see what we can find." From what he could gather, much of the western end of the Uinta Mountains was unroaded and relatively pristine country, accessible only to those willing to hike or go in on horseback. He'd seen no sign of anyone else in this area so far. "I've brought my thermal-image goggles to help us. Let's go."

They got out of the truck and she put on her backpack without waiting for his assistance. The more he got to know her, the more he noticed how independent she was, always protecting her body space. But there'd been a slight change in her from last week. Last evening he'd caught her staring at him a few times. That had to count for something. He planned to find out what during their hike.

Today there were clouds overhead, but they weren't threatening rain. When they blocked the sun, the forest air just grew cooler. The endless varieties of trees and undergrowth created a world of enchantment. Somewhere in this greenery a plantation of Early Misty marijuana was growing. He needed to stay focused to spot it, though Melissa's presence was a constant distraction.

The only sounds were of small animals and birds, and their own movements. For Travis it was as if they were the only two people on earth, encased in an almost spiritual solitude. He pitied anyone who'd never walked through a forest like this.

They'd been hiking for about two hours when he spotted movement in the distance. He stopped and waited until an elk with the biggest rack he'd ever seen walked into view. Signaling for Melissa to stop, he took off the goggles and helped her put them on. He stood behind her and pulled her against his chest while she took a good, long look.

"Oh, Travis," she whispered in awe, "he's magnificent. I think he must weigh a thousand pounds. Casey wouldn't believe it. I'd love to bring him hiking up here so he could see the elk, too."

"You'll have to draw him a picture," Travis suggested, speaking into her hair.

He felt a tremor run through her body, but she didn't move away. "I hope no hunter ever finds him."

"A rack that size proves he's eluded them for years."

Slowly, she peered around her, through the goggles. "I can see everything!" she exclaimed softly. She kept turning until she faced him. "There's nothing more beautiful than nature's creations."

"You're right." Without conscious thought he removed the goggles and set them down. "I'm looking at one of them right now. You have no idea how beautiful you are to me, Melissa." He'd loved watching her move quietly through the forest, a gorgeous human creature if there ever was one. His hands closed around her upper arms. "I want to kiss you, but you already know that."

"Because I look like your wife?" she asked with a daunting frankness.

He drew in a fortifying breath. "I don't know how to answer that. Maybe. Partly."

"That's honest, anyway. I can see in your eyes you'd give anything if I were her. But I'm me. I don't think you have any idea who *I* am."

His hands cupped her face. "Then there's only one

way to find out, isn't there?" He lowered his head and found her mouth with his own. It was sweet to the taste. So sweet. She'd been eating red grapes from her pack. He proceeded with slow deliberation, teasing her, pressing kisses against her throat and around her lips, invading her mouth a little deeper each time until she opened to him, like a rose opening to the sun.

He groaned before pulling her body to his. After Valerie, he'd thought he would never experience this kind of passion again. But holding Melissa in his arms, exploring her warm, pliant mouth, showed him he knew nothing about the mysterious alchemy stirring up his fire.

The world faded away as she wrapped her arms around his neck, allowing him to embrace her fully. He'd been craving this since she'd helped him put up cameras inside the cabin. While he'd been working, he'd had to fight the urge to reach out and touch her. Now he didn't have to hold back.

It wasn't his imagination that she wanted to get closer to him. Their bodies gravitated together in mutual need. One kiss didn't begin to satisfy and could never be enough for him. After such a long time in a state of limbo, the rapture he felt with this woman was almost beyond bearing. But it came to an abrupt end when she cried, "No, Travis!" and slid out of his arms.

He was so far gone, it took him a minute to realize what had just happened. Bereft after such ecstasy, he stood there breathing hard while he attempted to pull himself together. "What did I do that you didn't want me to?"

WITH THE CLOUDS SHUTTING out the sunlight, his eyes looked black. Melissa shook her head. "Nothing."

"But you wanted me. You were with me all the way."

"I don't deny it." Being in his arms, undergoing that explosion of joy when he'd kissed her breathless, had been a transcending experience Melissa had wanted to go on and on.

"Then what caused you to pull away? Did I frighten you?"

She rubbed her arms with her hands. "No…. Yes…. I don't know…."

He put his hands on his hips. "I *did* frighten you."

"No. It wasn't you. It's me. I frightened myself."

"Because you responded to me? Help me out here. I want to understand."

Melissa shook her head. "You had the power to make me respond when I had no intention of doing so."

"*Make* you? That's an odd choice of word. It takes two willing participants to feel what we were feeling."

"I don't want to talk about it. I—I can't," she stammered. "If you don't mind, I'd like to go back to the truck."

The safe world she'd created for herself since the divorce had just blown up in her face. For the first time in six years, she felt confused and out of control.

It was cruel to blame him for wanting his wife to still be alive. He could no more help it than he could fly. And Melissa knew it was sheer insanity to accuse him of trying to dominate her, when he'd done nothing of the kind. For days now she'd been wanting him to kiss her. Now that he had, she was a writhing mass of contradictions. She'd ruined it with him and could have bitten her tongue off for speaking to him like that.

Without saying anything, he put the goggles on again and started back the way they'd come, pacing his strides so she could keep up with him. When they got back to the truck, she checked her watch. It was one-thirty. They'd been out longer than she'd thought and they hadn't seen a soul.

He left her to remove her own pack and put it in the backseat. When she climbed into the cab, she still felt devastated by what she'd done. "Travis…I owe you an explanation, but I don't know where to start."

"You owe me nothing," he said in a remote tone of voice. "I felt like kissing you and I did, until you stopped me. We both know it happens to males and females all the time. It's just as well I got it out of my system so I can concentrate on finding the people invading your domain."

After starting the engine, he turned the truck around and they headed down the mountain. "I have to go to the cabin," he said, "so I can gather the memory cards from the cameras and put a new listening device in the flowers. I'll drive into Kamas and you can do some shopping there, or wait in the truck at the church, while I go up on foot. It won't take me long."

"I want to stay with you."

"I don't think so. Not after what happened back there."

"Please forget what I said." She was starting to panic.

"That would be impossible."

Melissa stirred restlessly. "I've made you angry, when it was the last thing I meant to do."

"If I'm angry, it's at myself. There's an unwritten law. No fraternizing with the clients. I've never crossed the line before and now I know why. Believe me, I won't do it again." The ice was back in his eyes.

She realized this wasn't the time to explain herself. He wasn't in a mood to listen. Perhaps by the time they reached the cabin, he'd be more approachable. For the rest of the drive to town she sat back and stared out the window, not seeing anything.

At one point his phone rang. He checked the caller ID before answering it. The call was a short one, but she sensed it was important. He didn't bother to explain, however.

When they reached Kamas, he parked at the church and said nothing as she headed up the road with him. But with every step, she grew more and more uncomfortable. Travis had surrounded himself with an invisible shield that no plea for leniency could penetrate.

Once at their destination, she followed him around the back. Melissa saw fresh cigarette butts outside the door the second he did.

He spoke at last. "There were more visitors here last night, but they didn't come from the area where we were hiking today. That leaves the section of forest I haven't explored yet."

He opened his pack to collect the samples and bag them. Returning to the front, he unlocked the door and they moved inside. "The lanterns have been transferred from the end table to the floor," she blurted.

"So I noticed. Your squatters have grown careless."

While Melissa drank water from the kitchen tap, he got busy removing the memory cards and replacing the batteries in the cameras. His last action was to hide a new listening device in the geraniums and pocket the other one.

"Shall we go?" he asked, his tone frigid.

She couldn't let things continue this way. The thought of trekking back to the truck and then driving down the canyon with him without saying a word was too painful to contemplate. In desperation she reached the front door ahead of him and flattened herself against it, so he'd have to remove her physically to go outside.

"We're not leaving until you let me explain."

His face was a study of lines and shadows. "It's not necessary."

"When I told you the reason for my divorce, I didn't tell you everything."

With that remark, he lifted his head. She had his attention. "Go on."

"Russ and I met in Kamas at the beginning of the summer. He was at his parents' summer home in Park City, and drove to Kamas with friends. We met at a local dance. He was good-looking, fun, funny, smart. He had lots of friends I really liked, and he liked my friends. I fell for him. In the fall, we got married."

Travis looked at her through veiled eyes. "What happened?"

"My parents had paid for my college education, and suggested that we wait and get another year of schooling behind us first, but we both wanted to marry. My siblings were married. All my friends were getting married. Love was in the air. I wanted what every girl wants, and didn't want to waste any more time. Mom and Dad got behind me, like they always do, and provided the beach honeymoon. It was great."

"You were still in love at the end of your honeymoon?"

"Yes. He was terrific to me and I assumed our wonderful lives would go on forever. Russ's father is a prominent, well-to-do Realtor, and he gave us a luxury house in an elegant neighborhood near the University of Utah for a wedding present. We had everything the upwardly mobile couple could ask for. Except for one thing I didn't see coming."

"What was that?"

"You've heard of Jekyll and Hyde."

Travis's features tautened. "How soon did he turn into Mr. Hyde?"

She averted her eyes, remembering the moment as if it was yesterday. "The day after our return from Laguna Beach. He wanted to control me." Her voice shook. "I'm not talking once in a while. I'm talking about every aspect of our lives. It was like a sickness."

"Why don't we sit down while you tell me the rest."

"I can't sit. Let me just tell you everything so you'll understand me better."

He folded his arms and stayed silent.

"Russ dictated when I went to bed, when I got up, what I cooked, what I ate," she stated numbly. "What I wore, what I did, where I went, what I read, who I did things with, how I spent his money. He curtailed the amount of time we spent with my family. He hated the cabin. He hated it when I painted. He chose what we watched on TV. When I was home from school, he checked on me all the time."

A pained expression crossed Travis's face, but he didn't interrupt.

"At first I thought I was living a nightmare. I prayed I would wake up, but it went on and on, and I knew I had to get out. But being beholden to both sets of parents, and knowing what our getting a divorce would do to them, I was afraid to tell them what was going on, afraid his parents would never believe me."

"You were trapped," Travis said with conviction. "I've seen it with other victims."

She nodded. "The only thing he couldn't control was my schoolwork and nursing classes. I immersed myself in my studies to stay mentally and emotionally away from him. I couldn't bear for him to touch me. One afternoon he came home while I was studying for midterms. He wanted to make love. The thought was so abhorrent to me, I did the only thing I could do, and told him I didn't have time.

"He got this crazed look in his eye and yanked me out of the chair. I tried to push him away, but he wouldn't take no for an answer and slapped me in the face, with such force, I fell to the floor."

"Melissa—"

"Luckily, when I got up, he saw that my cheek was all red and swelling, and he asked me to forgive me. He promised he'd never do it again." She swallowed hard. "I didn't give him the chance, and fled the house with my car keys."

"Thank heaven."

"The next day I filed for divorce. He didn't contest it. To my relief it went through without a hitch, and I never saw him again. But I heard he remarried, and it makes me ill for his new wife, just thinking about it."

Travis studied her for a tension-filled minute. "When I kissed you, it was the first time a man kissed you since your divorce, wasn't it?" His voice was low.

She drew in a deep breath. "I've dated a bit, but yes, you're the first."

His dark brows met in a frown. "And it brought that horrific moment back."

"No, that's not it. From the first time we met, I found myself attracted to you. When you told me I reminded you of your wife, I was utterly dismayed. Last night, when you watched me go in the town house, you said it was necessary because if you'd been on guard for your wife, she'd still be alive. To think that after six years I finally meet a man who appeals to me, and then I learn you only see Valerie when you look at me...

"On the drive up the canyon today, I told myself I was going to be strong and fight the attraction I felt. But when you told me you wanted to kiss me, that's what I wanted, too—more than anything. You know I did, and you know how much I enjoyed it. That's what I meant earlier when I said you had the power to make me respond when I had no intention of doing so. I lost control with you, but that was my problem, not yours."

Her explanation appeared to satisfy him. "So after giving in, why did you stop?"

"Because I remembered you were kissing *her,* not me. You were remembering your wife, and how you felt when she was in your arms. I could have gone on kissing you back, but I would have been lying to myself that it was me you really wanted."

He rubbed his jaw. "I can see that you and I both need more time together to dispel our ghosts from the past."

Melissa wished he hadn't said that. "I'm glad you feel that way," she whispered.

His gaze was centered on her mouth, causing hers to tingle in response. "We'd better get going. I have to drop off the latest samples at the lab before I pick up Casey."

"I'm ready."

Together they left the cabin. Unburdening herself turned out to be cathartic. By the time they reached the truck in town, Melissa felt a lightening of her spirit.

Once they were sitting in the cab, he gave her a searching glance. "Tell me something," he said. "Were you reminded of your ex-husband when the employee at Grampy's leered at you?"

She nodded.

"When you went pale like you did, I knew you'd been deeply disturbed."

"No wonder you Texas Rangers are so legendary. Nothing gets by you."

His disarming smile chased away her earlier fear that she might never see it again. "Let's hope that holds true during my investigation." He pulled the listening device from his pocket. "We know from those fresh cig-

arette butts that someone was in your cabin last night.
I'm curious to hear what this picked up." He turned it
on so they could both listen.

She heard a number of male voices. That alone made
her shudder—to think a bunch of men were in the cabin's kitchen as if they owned the place. Melissa listened
more intently. "They're all speaking Spanish. Do you
understand what they're saying?"

"I can pick out a little, but they're not conversing
in the kind of Spanish I used to hear in Texas. This is
a fast-paced dialect with certain phonetic changes I'm
unfamiliar with. I'll need Jose for this. He's our expert."

Melissa watched Travis turn off the device and put
it in his pocket. "What are you thinking?"

"This and that."

"Travis—" she half moaned in frustration "—that
was one of your nonanswers again."

His jaw hardened. "After I get back to the office, I'll
look through the camera memory cards and will know
a lot more. Once I've pieced everything together, I'll
tell you my suspicions."

He didn't have to say it; a bunch of men up to no
good had to be armed and dangerous.

He switched on the ignition. On the way out of town
he stopped in front of the Quickie Mart. "I have to go inside, but I'll only be a minute. Do you want anything?"

"No, thank you."

Maybe he needed to use the restroom, Melissa decided. But with him you never could tell, because he op-
erated on his own private agenda. Whatever was going
on, the tension was building.

TRAVIS ENTERED THE MART, where he'd arranged to meet Jose back by the cold drinks section. His friend had driven up in the R & T Painting Company truck from the P.I. shop. It had been parked alongside a dozen other vehicles. There were still a lot of tourists on vacation.

When Travis found him, he was dressed in a painter's overalls and cap. They both reached for a Coke. Travis took a second one in case Melissa wanted one. "What did you find out so far?"

"The same man and a woman I tailed Tuesday showed up at Grampy's for work at five to ten. They drove the same cars as before. I checked with the DMV and found out there's no police record or warrants out on them. Both driving records are clean.

"Our man with the tattoo left the camper on foot and arrived at Grampy's at eleven. I'll watch till he goes off shift and follow him again. When I find out anything else, I'll let you know."

Travis nodded. "I'll check to see if those fingerprints taken at the cabin produce results. Who knows? We might get lucky and some names will turn up, his among them. You've got enough backup?"

"Plenty."

"Good. When you've got a minute, listen to this and give me your expert opinion." He handed him the listening device. "I pulled it from the flowers in the kitchen."

"I'll do it as soon as I get back in the truck."

"Thanks."

Travis went to the checkout stand first to pay for his drinks, then joined Melissa in the truck. "I bought you a Coke."

"Thank you."

On the way down the canyon he decided to share some information with her. He was aware he'd been secretive, yet she never asked about the case. That was a quality he respected in her more than she could possibly realize.

"I went in the mart to meet up with Jose and give him the listening device. He'll translate for me when he gets a chance."

She nodded. "You don't do anything without a reason."

They had just emerged from the canyon when Jose phoned. Travis picked up. "What's new?"

Jose whistled, and that alone told him plenty. "Give me five minutes and I'll call you back," Travis suggested.

"It's probably a good idea you're alone when I tell you."

He didn't like the sound of that. "Understood."

He drove straight to Melissa's town house and pulled up in front. She climbed out in a hurry and retrieved her pack from the backseat.

"Casey and I will be over at six to get you," he said.

"You still want me to come?" She looked anxious.

"At the cabin I thought we agreed we needed to get to know each other better. Or have you changed your mind?"

"No," she said quickly. "No. But let me come to you. Give me directions to your house and I'll be there at six, okay?"

He agreed. And her positive response relieved him.

They had things to work out. After she'd unburdened herself today, he feared she'd retreat emotionally before they got to know each other better. Travis didn't think he could handle that. Much to his surprise, he recognized she was becoming important to his existence.

And he realized that he was seeing Melissa in her own right and not as a clone of Valerie. In time he hoped to prove it to her.

"Okay, see you later."

She nodded. After she'd gone inside the condo, he pulled out his phone and rang Jose. "Go ahead and tell me what you heard. I'm alone now."

"It's all coming together, Travis. Those men in the cabin are from Colombia. I counted four distinct voices. They're speaking the Choquano dialect from the northern coastal region. They talked about the hard work and the isolation. One of them said the pay was going to be great, so stop complaining. Another talked about finding women when this was over. They were getting tired of the job.

"One complained of a bad toothache. Another guy said he was going to jump the woman whose bedroom was upstairs before they cleared out. He described in detail what he wanted to do to her. His friend suggested they wait to get paid, then kidnap her. She would be of interest to the boss, who'd want her for himself.

"It could be worth a lot of extra *dinero* for them if they took her back with them, he said. Her family wouldn't know what had happened to her, and would never be able to find her. There was laughter and then silence."

Rage curled Travis's hands into fists. The mention of their plans for Melissa twisted his gut. If Casey hadn't told her about Travis's job while they were at the movie, she might not have sought help soon enough to avoid the fate awaiting her. At least he could be thankful that Valerie hadn't been molested before she was killed.

"Travis?" Jose said in concern. "Are you all right?"

Travis struggled for breath. "No. And I won't be until these vermin are caught and put away in prison to rot. If this is a big operation like the one on Boulder Mountain, then there's a lot more at stake and we're dealing with men who'll kill to protect their crop."

"Which means there's a lot of money behind them."

"I've got my work cut out finding those plants, so we'll know exactly what we're up against. Let's hope the next recording gives us some kind of time line for their activities. With it being mid-September, they have to be coming to the end of the harvest."

"Agreed. I'm here on surveillance when you want to talk."

The call ended. Travis dropped off the new samples at the lab, then swung by the school to pick up Casey. In a couple of hours they'd be seeing Melissa again. He could hardly wait.

Chapter Eight

Melissa followed Travis's directions to his house in the Lone Peak Estates and pulled up in front. She loved the country-cottage-style home on sight. White trim enhanced the stone exterior and matched the white fencing.

Casey answered her knock. Apparently Travis was tied up on the phone, so Casey and Dexter took her on the grand tour. Dark honey flooring ran from the foyer throughout the downstairs. The mix of traditional and contemporary furnishings reflecting the wood tones against soft yellow walls gave the interior a warm, livable feel.

She accompanied Casey into the formal dining room with its decorative columns. It led to the two-story great room with a stone fireplace, and beyond it, the kitchen and breakfast room done in sage accents.

He then led her to their bedrooms at the rear of the house. At the first one he announced, "This is my room."

She could tell. It had everything a boy could want. "I love it, especially your posters of Spider-Man and Optimus Prime."

But there was something else she loved more: the framed photograph of his father in his Texas Ranger uniform hanging over the bed. Travis looked younger in the picture and handsome as sin.

Her gaze darted to more family photographs propped on his dresser. Casey took one and showed it to Melissa. It was a head shot of his mother, wearing a crew-neck top like the one Melissa had worn today.

She gasped, seeing the smiling woman. They *did* have definite similarities. In this picture, her light brown hair was pulled back the way Melissa's was. It revealed the tiny blue sparkling jewels in her ears that matched her blue-gray eyes. Eyes like Melissa's.

To see this photo of his wife, after hearing of their likeness, explained so much about Travis's initial reaction to Melissa at the clinic. She put it back on the dresser before looking at Casey.

"You must miss her very much."

His sigh spoke volumes. "Yup, but she's gone to heaven. You're nice and pretty, just like her. I wish you lived with us all the time."

Melissa moaned inwardly, while her throat swelled. "Thank you, Casey," she whispered, knowing she didn't dare tell him the same thing back. "That's the greatest compliment I ever received." She couldn't deal with the pain any longer. "Shall we finish the tour?"

"Okay. Come on, Dexter."

They went to Travis's bedroom, which had a coffered ceiling and luxurious bath. Melissa didn't stay to look around for other pictures of his wife.

There were two more bedrooms at the top of a

white staircase. The house was utterly charming, but she found the real character of their home came from the prints and two oil paintings hanging on the walls. Casey said they'd brought them from Texas. The big one in the dining room showed a field of gorgeous Texas bluebonnets.

The other oil, a very large one in the great room, showed a black stallion racing ahead of some other horses. It was obviously a favorite, and had been signed. The artist had caught the beauty and swiftness of horses in motion. From experience Melissa knew it was a hard thing to capture.

"This is fabulous," she told Travis as he walked into the room.

He studied it for minute. "Before Casey and I left Texas, the Rangers in my district took up a collection to buy this for me. The artist is becoming famous. Nothing could have surprised or pleased me more." His voice was thick with emotion.

Tears stung her eyelids, but she refused to cry. "They must have thought the world of you. Did you ride a lot?"

"All my life. Mostly for pleasure, sometimes on the job."

"Are your parents still living, Travis?"

"No," Casey answered for him. "They were killed by a train when he and Aunt Pat were babies. Their truck stalled on the track and they couldn't get out in time."

Melissa gulped. "That's awful."

"I know. My grandpa was a Texas Ranger, too!"

"I didn't know that."

"Yup. Daddy and Aunt Pat had to go live with their aunt and uncle."

"And we were very fortunate," Travis confided. "They became our parents and they were horse people. After my aunt May passed away from a lung clot, it was just the three of us. When Uncle Frank died of a heart attack, Pat and I inherited their house and lived in it."

Casey nodded. "And then Aunt Pat got married and moved to Salt Lake, and then Daddy met Mommy and they got married."

Melissa smiled at Travis's adorable boy. "And then *you* came along. That was a really lucky day for your parents."

Sadness tinged his smile. "I didn't want to move to Salt Lake, but now I'm glad we did. Do you ride horses?"

After their little talk in the bedroom, she realized where this was leading. "I have done. There's a stable in Kamas where you can go for rides, but I'm not very good. Are you thinking of getting horses again?"

"Maybe," Travis said. "We're taking this one step at a time."

No doubt he'd ridden with his wife. After her death he'd probably lost his love for it. Certainly Casey's recent fall wouldn't put him in any hurry to do something about it.

"Who's ready for dinner?" Travis asked. "Our Chinese food arrived while you two were touring the house."

"I don't like that stuff," Casey said in dismay.

"I made you mac and cheese, bud."

Melissa grinned. "And I brought you more home-made brownies."

"Yippee!"

TRAVIS CAME IN the breakfast room after putting Casey to bed. While they were gone, she'd cleaned up the kitchen. He brought his laptop with him and sat down at the table. From his pocket he pulled out the three tiny micro SD cards taken from the mini cameras.

Melissa looked at him. "Is Casey asleep?"

"Not yet, but I think he's on the way."

Suddenly, they said each other's name, at the exact same time. "You go first," Travis told her.

"Casey showed me a picture of his mother. I—I can see why you were taken back when we first met." Melissa's voice faltered.

"I didn't know you then."

"Still—"

"Still, nothing." He cut her off. "Even identical twins have differences when you get to know them."

"All I'm trying to say is that I'm not so sure Casey has made that distinction."

"Does it matter?" Travis watched her fidget.

"It might. That's why I made up the excuse about doing the dishes instead of going in his room to read him a bedtime story. I don't think it's wise that I get any closer to him."

"Are you sure you're not talking about me instead of my son?"

"Travis, please listen to me. After talking about his

mother, he told me he wished I lived with you all the time."

"That shouldn't surprise you." It had become Casey's mantra.

"No, but it troubles me. When you told me about his immediate turnaround after coming to the clinic, I only halfway believed your explanation. Not because I thought you were lying, but because it sounded so unlikley."

"But now you know it's true. So what if it is? Why are you so worried about it?"

She eyed him in confusion. "Because he has unrealistic expectations. One day, when I don't meet them, he's going to be let down."

"I haven't seen any sign of it."

"You're not hearing what I'm saying."

"I am hearing you. We both know he's transferred his feelings for his mom to you."

"Yes, but I'm not his mom, and when he eventually realizes it, his disappointment could present problems."

Travis had known the day would come when Melissa saw Valerie's picture. Now that she had, she'd started doubting him, fearing he couldn't separate his feelings about the two of them any more than Casey could. In fact, she was making sounds about wanting to distance herself from him as well.

Travis refused to allow that to happen before they could explore what was going on between them. Those kisses in the forest had been earthshaking for him.

"Then we'll deal with them if and when that time comes, okay?"

He stared her down. At last she gave him a small smile. "Okay," she said.

"Good. Right now we have a case to solve. Let's take a look at these tapes and see what's on them. This one is from the back door outside the cabin." He inserted the first memory card into the adaptor so they could view it on the laptop, full screen. "The time indicated says ten fifty-five."

"What on earth are they doing out in the forest so late at night?"

"I'm working on the answer." Travis knew exactly what they were doing. Tomorrow he'd hike with Melissa over the ridge in the other direction. In all likelihood he'd find what he was looking for, otherwise these drug traffickers wouldn't be using her family's cabin rather than some cheap motel miles from there.

Out of the darkness came the beam of a flashlight, moving around like a firefly. Melissa gasped as she counted one, two, three, four silhouettes coming toward the camera before they disappeared into the cabin.

"How dare they!" she said, appalled.

Travis picked up another memory card and put it in. "This one will be from the upstairs camera. It says ten after eleven." Again there was movement of a flashlight beam, followed by two silhouettes climbing the staircase.

Melissa shook her head. "How convenient! A bedroom for each of them."

"They probably had another one on watch outside the cabin, in case they had to get out in a hurry, but the camera didn't catch him. That might explain the number of cigarette butts."

He removed the card and put in the next. "Ten fifty-six." The tape caught the backs of four men in long-sleeved jackets entering the kitchen, one still wielding a flashlight. The man holding it put it on the picnic table, while they all crowded around the sink for a drink from the tap. They didn't use glasses from the cupboard. In another minute they assembled on the benches in the kitchen.

Melissa glanced at Travis. "Judging by the look of them, they're all Hispanic. That certainly explains why we heard Spanish on the listening device."

He nodded. "When Jose translated the audio, he picked up four voices, all of them native speakers." That was as much as he was willing to tell her.

"What were they talking about?"

"How hungry and thirsty they were. One had a toothache."

"But nothing about what they were doing in the mountains?"

"Not yet. But when we go up to the cabin tomorrow, I'll put in yet another listening device, and hope we pick up more chatter."

"Tomorrow's Friday. They might not come, since it'll be the weekend."

"We'll just have to wait and see. I plan to come by for you at eight-thirty in the morning. We'll spend the day up there. I'll ask Deana to pick Casey up from school, so it will give us a little more time to hike."

All of a sudden there was movement on the tape. The

kitchen became shrouded in darkness as one of the men took the flashlight and got up from the table. Another left with him, presumably to go upstairs. Which meant the other two were left in the dark. When there was nothing more to see, Travis pulled out the memory card.

Melissa shot up from the table. "I can't wait till they're caught. They sicken me. About a month ago I was watching an old Hollywood war movie where the enemy shot everyone inside this gorgeous French château before they took it over. It was winter. They chopped up the furniture and parquet floors for firewood.

"Some of the soldiers used the fabulous Sèvres china urns for chamber pots. They showed no mercy or regard for anything. I know it was just a movie, but it was based on a thousand true stories. I remembered thinking, what if that were my family? Our château? Now I have an inkling what it feels like for an enemy to invade your home as if it's their divine right."

Travis reached for her and wrapped his arms around her. She didn't resist. "I'm so close to catching them, I can taste it." He kissed her cheek and hair. "Bear with me a little longer and I promise you'll soon be rid of them for good."

"You think I don't know that?" she cried into his neck. "What if Casey hadn't told me you were a P.I.? It's a miracle you've already unearthed so much. Who else but a Texas Ranger could do what you've done?"

The warmth of her body proved to be an aphrodisiac that drove everything else from Travis's mind. He kissed his way to her mouth and began devouring her.

His hunger for her had been building. Whatever reservations she had about him seemed to have dissolved, because she was soon kissing him back with a fervency that matched his own.

He had no idea how long they stood there, locked in a feverish embrace. But when Dexter's bark registered, Travis realized they were no longer alone. Melissa had heard it, too, and eased out of his arms. He noticed her flushed face and swollen lips before he turned to discover Casey standing nearby. His son's blue eyes stared at them with a soberness that was puzzling, and he didn't say anything.

"What are you still doing up, bud?"

"I couldn't sleep."

Travis sighed. "Maybe it's just as well. I was going to ask your aunt to walk across the street and keep you company while I followed Melissa home. Now you can come with me. Stay in your pj's, but put some shoes on. Then we'll leave."

"I'll be right back!" Casey took off with Dexter at his heels.

Knowing this wasn't the time for a postmortem with Melissa, Travis escorted her through the house and out the front door to her car. After helping her inside, he leaned down for another taste of her divine mouth.

"Travis…Casey can see us." She tore her lips from his, but not before he'd felt her respond. It gratified him to know her emotions were spilling over, too.

He kissed her nose. "We'll be right behind you."

When Travis unlocked the truck, Casey and Dexter climbed in the back. On the way over to Melissa's the boy was still unusually quiet. Travis eyed him through the rearview mirror. "What's on your mind?"

"I don't think Melissa likes me."

That was a surprise. "Where did you get an idea like that? I seem to recall she's given you lots of presents, and she made more brownies for you tonight."

"I know."

"So what's the problem?"

A haunting sigh escaped before he murmured, "I told her I wished she lived with us all the time."

Travis rubbed his jaw. "What did she say?"

Silence greeted his question. They were almost to Melissa's town house, so Travis prodded, "Casey?"

"She didn't say anything," he answered in a quiet voice.

Travis's earlier conversation with Melissa had come back to bite him. "That doesn't mean she doesn't like you. You have to remember Melissa isn't your mother. She's never been a mother," he said in a burst of inspiration, wanting to help his son get past this hurt.

"You mean she doesn't know how?" Casey sounded as if he couldn't imagine such a thing. It made Travis smile despite the pang in his heart.

"Yeah, that's what I mean. And guess what? *I* didn't know how to be a father until after I got married and you were born. Your mom and I learned how together."

He could hear the wheels turning in Casey's head.

"Do you think if you married Melissa, you could teach her and she'd learn how?"

Travis didn't reply.

MELISSA WAS PACKING hard-boiled eggs and peanut butter sandwiches in her backpack when her phone rang. Maybe it was Travis calling to tell her he was going to be late picking her up. Instead it was her sister.

"Linda?"

"Hi! I know, it's been at least two weeks since I last talked to you. Dad said you've taken the week off and we shouldn't go up to the cabin until the P.I. figures out what's going on. I want to hear all about what's happening up there, but first I need a favor."

"What?"

"My babysitter can't come at eleven, and I have an appointment with my ob-gyn for my annual pap smear. I was wondering if you might be able to help me out. I know it's late notice."

"You know I would in a second, but the guy heading the investigation is coming by for me in a few minutes. We have to go up the canyon again. I'm so sorry."

"Hey, it's all right. I'll call Mom. I hate to ask her, but sometimes there isn't anything else to do. If that fails, I'll cancel the appointment. So how's it going? Do you trust this P.I. to know what he's doing?"

Heat swept through Melissa. The memory of the way Travis had kissed her in his kitchen last night had kept her awake for hours. "He's brilliant."

"Really. Is he young? Old?"

"Mid-thirties."

"Married?"

"Linda...not you, too! Mom and Dad do enough of that."

"I'm getting warmer, aren't I? You've been so quiet lately, something tells me he's a person of interest."

"He hopes to have the case solved soon. That's the only thing of interest to me."

"Liar. But I'm glad to hear you have such confidence in him. One of these days I want the inside skinny on him. In the meantime I'm sure you can't wait to get the cabin back. I know you'd live up there if you could."

"You know me too well." Except that since Melissa had met Travis, she couldn't imagine being up there without him.

"Well, I'd better try phoning Mom. We'll talk later. Have a good day!"

"You, too."

After they hung up, Melissa put her keys in her pocket and left the condo carrying her backpack. Travis was out in front, right on time. She felt an adrenaline rush, something that happened every time she saw him. As she deposited her backpack in the rear and climbed into the truck, she sensed his mind was somewhere else. Whether it was personal or work-related, she couldn't tell.

Probably he was thinking about those men they'd seen on the video, who had to be close to the cabin. Maybe today would be the day she and Travis would catch sight of them, though they'd be hiking in a rugged area she hadn't been in since she was a kid. Still, two pairs of eyes were better than one.

She put on her best smile and said, "Good morning." When he turned to her, his gaze traveled over her and centered on her mouth. "It is now. But I'm having second thoughts about taking you with me."

And here she'd hoped he might kiss her. What was she thinking? "Why?"

"I've decided you'll be safer here."

She frowned. "I thought you had backup for us."

"I do, but even with the best-laid plans, things can go wrong. I'd prefer not to take any chances."

"Why don't you tell me what's really wrong? You think I'll slow you down?"

"You know better than that."

"So how about telling me the truth?"

His jaw tensed. "This has to do with Casey."

She bit her lip. "Is he all right?"

"He won't be if anything happens to you."

Melissa stared at Travis, trying hard to read between the lines. "What you're not saying is that this case has escalated into something highly explosive. Am I right?"

"I'm afraid so. On the way over here, Jose called me from the cabin. The men were there again last night, and he overheard conversation on the listening device that has required us to step up the operation. Now the police are involved."

"So that means the Texas Ranger is once again walking into a situation that could take lives."

"Not if I can help it." His voice was hard.

Melissa felt real fear. "I wish I'd never told my father about the Lufka firm."

"Thank heaven you did," Travis retorted.

"Why?" she cried.

He grimaced. "Never mind."

Now she was terrified. "Travis, if anything happened to you, Casey would never be able to handle the loss, and I'd never be able to forgive myself." *I'd never get over it.*

"If you're home safe and sound at least I'll be able to concentrate on the job I've got to do. Promise me you'll stay put today. I'll call you before the day is out. I swear it."

Melissa's heart pounded so hard she felt ill. "What about Casey?"

"Deana will pick him up from school. If I can't get home tonight, my sister's going to take care of him."

This was a crisis, but Travis wasn't asking for Melissa's help.

Was that because she'd told him she didn't dare get too close to Casey?

Or had he decided it was best to maintain distance because he'd finally separated her from his wife and she didn't stand up to the comparison?

Whatever the answer, he didn't want her around. Melissa got the message. "Sorry for holding you up." She jumped out of the truck and reached in back for her pack.

"Melissa..." His blue eyes glittered.

"Whatever you do, come home to your son," she said. And without waiting for a response, she raced up the sidewalk to her condo and let herself in. Once safely locked inside, she ran to her room and collapsed on the bed in a paroxysm of tears.

When she finally couldn't sob any longer, she got up and washed her face. After that she left the town house and drove to her sister's home in the Sugar House area of Salt Lake, not far from the university. Melissa wanted the comfort of Linda's toddlers. If her mother came over, so much the better. She'd never needed her family more.

CASEY HAD BEEN IN Travis's heart from the second they'd learned Valerie was pregnant. But recently someone else had joined his son in that secret chamber. Melissa wasn't happy about his decision this morning, but he would no longer subject her to the dangers awaiting her at the cabin.

When it came to his work, he'd learned to separate his personal life from the mission at hand. There was no other way to survive.

On his trip up the canyon he received a call from Roman. "Travis, I just talked to the detective at police headquarters about the fingerprints you lifted at the cabin. The one taken off the pine table was a match for the prints found at the crime scene in Douglas, Arizona, of that elderly couple. It's the man you fingered at Grampy's."

"That had to be a one-in-a-million shot. I can't believe it paid off."

"It's more like a billion. I'd bet on your vibes anytime, comrade. There's more. The left front tire on the camper has the two cuts that showed up on the tire tape at forensics. That puts him at the cabin, to provide the link. One more thing, Travis. He's on the FBI's Most Wanted list. I'm afraid he's right up there with your wife's killer," Roman said in a quieter voice. "At least you have one of them in your sights, and he won't be getting away."

Adrenaline shot through Travis. "What does his rap sheet look like?"

"It's a mile long. His name is Luis Manuel Carvelo."

"He didn't sound or look Hispanic."

"He's probably mixed blood and bilingual. As for his hair, he bleaches it. But his earlier photo shows him with black hair, slicked back. He's wanted for unlawful flight to avoid prosecution, murder, kidnapping, rape and parole violation. In July of 2010 he shot and killed three gang members in Holbrook, Arizona. A year later he kidnapped, raped and murdered a woman in Lake Havasu.

"Carvelo is believed to work for a Colombian drug cartel, and is known to travel between the U.S. and Colombia via Mexico. His rap sheet says he may have a tattoo on the back of his neck—and with you on the case, we know he does. You're a great asset, Travis."

"It works both ways."

"The Feds are ready to move in as soon as you give the signal."

That moment couldn't come too soon for Travis. Jose's latest information via the listening device confirmed what he'd been worried about: the illegals had indicated the coming weekend would be the end of the harvest. By next week they'd have made a haul worth millions on the streets.

It was now or never for Travis. He had to find the marijuana grove while the men were still working it. Otherwise they'd move on and start another plantation somewhere else, and the culprits would slip through his fingers.

"I hope to have news by nightfall."

"Be careful."

"Always."

Travis clicked off and turned onto another firebreak road that gave him access to an area he needed to explore. After climbing out of his truck and locking it, he moved into the shadows of the forest and began hiking quickly. This side of the mountain was definitely steeper. It would be a difficult climb to the mine Melissa had mentioned. Even if gold wasn't what the Colombians were after, it might have been, under other circumstances.

Armed with his heat-seeking goggles, Travis zigzagged up the slope. He'd been walking about ten minutes when his boot tip hit something that pitched him forward, straight into a crop of Early Misty marijuana.

Travis leaned over to find black pipes hidden among the plants, evidence of an elaborate irrigation system. He followed it a few hundred yards to a narrow stream. Careful now, he waded through the twists and turns. At a certain vantage point his goggles picked up human forms. He counted six men working above him. One of them was Carvelo.

After the way the killer had eyed Melissa when she'd walked up to the window at Grampy's, there was no doubt in Travis's mind he was the man who'd had plans for her. *It's not going to happen, you monster.*

Reaching for his camera, Travis took shots of the entire area including the makeshift camp. He saw a couple of rifles propped against a log. Obviously, the illegals were prepared to fight off other traffickers who might want the same rewards.

There were natural springs and hundreds of feet of irrigation piping, with sprinklers to water the plants. Garbage was strewn everywhere, including containers of fertilizer and other chemicals.

It was difficult to guess how many thousands of plants were under cultivation, but Travis had no doubt some of the crap had already been harvested. This close to the firebreak road, it would be easy to haul it off in trucks, with no one the wiser. The Feds would get aerial photographs to identify the perimeter.

Having seen all he needed to see, Travis made a bee-line to his truck before it was spotted. On the way down to Kamas, he phoned Roman. "Tell the Feds they can move in. I hit the jackpot. There are six men, Carvelo among them. They're armed. Here are the coordinates."

"I'll relay this to Jose and Lon. They're on their way up. Anything you need, let us know," his boss told him.

"I'm going to park my truck away from the firebreak road, then hike back up and watch for signs of trucks pulling near the camp to pick up the marijuana," he repeated. "I'll get license plate numbers and pictures."

Travis had a personal reason for wanting to see this whole operation go down fast. When it was over, he couldn't wait to see the look on Melissa's face when he told her she had her cabin back to enjoy. And then he couldn't wait to get her alone and make certain things clear to her.

Chapter Nine

Melissa's mother joined her at Linda's house, and they spent the whole day together with the children. After her sister got back from her doctor's appointment, the three of them were able to visit. It gave Melissa a chance to tell them everything she knew about what was happening at the cabin.

Though they were horrified, Melissa assured them that Travis had kept her perfectly safe, and it wouldn't be long before he caught the bad guys. When she told them he was a former Texas Ranger whose wife had been murdered in a revenge killing, the tone of the conversation changed. There couldn't be any question in her loved ones' minds that Travis was of vital importance to her, but for once Linda didn't tease her and her mother didn't pry.

When it got to be seven o'clock, Melissa drove home to her condo, half expecting Travis would have called her by now. Finally the phone rang. She picked up without looking at the caller ID.

"Hello?"

"Is this Melissa Dalton?"

"Yes?" She didn't recognize the voice.

"This is Pat Lawrence, Travis's sister."

"Oh, hello! He's told me wonderful things about you and your family."

"I've heard a lot of good things about you, too, and hope you don't mind my phoning."

"Not at all." Melissa's pulse raced. "Did he call you?"

"No. Travis gave me your phone number this morning before he left for the mountains. He indicated he might not get home before tomorrow, or even the next day. Realizing how Casey worries when he's late, Travis said you would know how to comfort him."

It meant the world to Melissa that Travis trusted her enough to provide backup in case of an emergency. "Is Casey anxious now?"

"He has that solemn look on his face. A few minutes ago he asked if he could talk to you."

"Oh, of course he can."

"All right. Just a minute and I'll get him."

Her heart was racing by the time he came to the phone. "Melissa?"

"Hi, sweetheart. How are you doing?"

"Have you heard from my dad?" He was worried, all right. Otherwise he would have answered her question, if only to tell her what Dexter was up to.

"No, but I do know he's working hard on the case. Just remember he has a whole backup team that works with him, so they keep each other safe."

"I know," the little boy said in a subdued voice. "I want to go home. Could you come to my house and stay with me till he gets there?"

He wants me, rather than his aunt? Melissa's throat

swelled with emotion. "Of course. I'll come now. Do you have a key?"

"Yup."

"Great. When you see my Jeep in the driveway, then run across the street."

"Okay. See ya!" He ended their conversation on a happier note.

Since it was possible Travis wouldn't be home until tomorrow or even the next day, she pulled out an overnight bag and packed the clothes and toiletries she'd need. On top of them she put in some of her art supplies and her portfolio. Casey might like to look through it.

Before long she'd left her condo and driven the short distance to Lone Peak Estates. No sooner had she pulled into the driveway than Travis's sister walked Casey across the street. Dexter came running up to Melissa while the two women shook hands and chatted. They all went inside Travis's house. Casey hurried to his room to put on his pajamas.

"I brought enough clothes to stay through the weekend if I have to," Melissa confided. "Travis has been setting up a sting. I'm presuming it could take several days."

"The idea was that when he moved here and took the P.I. job, he'd be in less danger. But we both know it's *all* dangerous."

Melissa eyed Pat, who resembled her brother and was very attractive. "At the movie, Casey told me his dad went after bad guys. I think it's what Travis was born to do."

"I *know* it was."

"For what it's worth, I have total confidence in him," Melissa said. "There's an authority about him. That picture of him over Casey's bed says it all. Travis has no idea how much I admire him." The throb in her voice had to be a giveaway.

Casey's aunt studied Melissa for a moment. "You're so different than Valerie."

"You're kidding! According to Travis, if you don't look too closely, I'm a dead ringer for her."

"You have similar coloring, but you're nothing alike. She was terrified of the work he did. In fact, she was so scared she begged him to quit after every case. It was a constant source of trouble between them. They almost divorced over it."

This was news to Melissa. Somehow she had this idea everything had been perfect between them. "I didn't realize."

"My brother has gone through hell believing that if he'd gotten out of the Rangers, she'd still be alive. But as I've reminded him, not every man is lucky enough to love what he does and be a natural at it. In Texas he's a hero to many people."

"He's a hero to our family," Melissa confessed emotionally. "Thank heaven he went to work for Lufka's. You should see how fast and thoroughly he set things up at the cabin that first day. I never saw anything like it in my life!"

"He can't stay away from what he knows and does best. Of course it's tragic that Valerie was killed, but none of us has a guarantee in this life. Our own parents were killed by a train."

Melissa nodded. "Casey told me."

"I'd better get home," Pat whispered, as her young nephew came running in the kitchen. "Call me if you need anything."

"Of course. We'll keep in touch."

"Good night, Casey." Pat kissed the top of his head and left the house.

"Will you sleep with me tonight?" the boy asked.

"Sure. Let's go to your room and I'll change into my jammies."

"What kind are they?"

"I don't have Spider-Man. Mine are just navy sweats."

"Oh."

They walked to his bedroom at the rear of the house. She disappeared into the bathroom. When she came out, she'd removed the combs from her hair and was wearing it loose, so she could give it a good brushing.

"Wow! I've never seen your hair like that before! You look different."

She guessed she did. "Don't you like it down?" It touched the top of her shoulders.

"I *love* it. You should wear it that way all the time."

"Well, thank you for the compliment. Why don't you pick out a couple of your favorite books? After you say your prayers, we'll read until we fall asleep."

"Hooray!"

A half hour later they pulled up the covers. Dexter crept into the space between them.

"Night, Melissa. I love you," Casey sighed.

Hot tears trickled from the corners of her eyes. "I love you, too. Sleep tight."

AT SIX IN THE MORNING Travis pulled into the driveway. His heart thudded when he discovered Melissa's Jeep there. He came to a stop and closed his eyes tightly. Casey must have asked Pat to call her or Melissa wouldn't be here. He exhaled a sigh of gratitude that they were both safe inside.

There was so much to tell her. Now he wouldn't have to go over to her house tomorrow to talk to her, or track her down if she wasn't there.

He tried to be quiet as he let himself in the front door, but Dexter was right there to greet him. Travis picked him up and carried him through the house. He passed Casey's bedroom and saw two heads against the pillows, sound asleep. Half a dozen books lay on the floor. What a sight!

"You're going to spend the rest of the night with me," Travis told Dexter, after he'd shut the door to his own bedroom. He set the Scottie down. Taking a few more steps, he fell across his bed, dirty and exhausted.

Nothing else registered until he felt a nudge on his shoulder. Light filled the room.

"Daddy? Wake up. Melissa's fixing us dinner."

Dinner? "What time is it?"

"Five o'clock."

Travis's lids opened. Through bleary eyes he saw his son, and pulled him into his arms. It was so wonderful getting back to normal! He rolled Casey on his back and tickled him until he begged him to stop.

"Hey, what's all that black on you?"

Travis could just imagine what he looked like after the night he'd lived through. "I guess I should take a shower, huh?"

"You need a shave, too. It scratches."

Travis saw movement in the doorway, but almost didn't recognize Melissa with her hair down and flowing around her shoulders. Talk about a vision.

"Welcome back." She smiled. "This room smells like there's been a fire in here. Come on, Casey. While your father does what he has to do to make himself presentable—if that's possible—we'll get dinner on the table."

Travis grinned at her. "That bad, huh?"

She nodded. "Pretty awful. Even Dexter didn't want to stay in here any longer."

Travis barked a laugh. "How come you're not running away?"

"I don't know. There must be something about you, but I'll have to think about it," she teased.

"Give me five minutes."

"Take ten, *please.*"

More laughter rolled out of him. After everyone disappeared, he got out of bed and stretched before going into his bathroom to shower. One look at his soiled clothes convinced him they'd need two to three washings to get clean again.

He hurriedly showered and shaved, then pulled on clean jeans and a sport shirt. When he emerged from his room, the smell of Italian food drew him to the breakfast room. Melissa and Casey must have gone to the grocery store during the day. The dinner she had prepared made him salivate. Along with lasagna, there was a fruit salad dotted with fat strawberries and daubs of whipped cream.

Travis sat down at the table, trapping her gaze. "This all looks so good, I don't know where to dig in first."

"Try these bread sticks!" Casey blurted, eating one as fast as he could. "Melissa made them all by herself. She let me twist them."

"I'd say you did a great job." Travis reached for one and ate it in two seconds. "You could make a whole meal of these."

"Hey, Dad," Casey said. "How come you got so dirty?"

"I was just going to ask you the same question," Melissa said.

He checked his watch. "It's almost five-thirty. If we turn on the TV to Channel Five, you'll get your answer."

"TV? I'll do it!" Casey slid out of his chair and ran over to the portable on the counter. When he switched it on, the local announcers were talking about a truck that had overturned near Saint George on I-15, and thousands of bees in their hives had spilled out onto the freeway. Beekeepers had to be sent for to clear up the mess.

"Uh-oh," Travis said. "I hope Abby doesn't see this."

"She'll freak out!" Casey exclaimed.

"Who's Abby?" Melissa said.

"One of our friends, huh, Daddy? She got stung by a bee and now she's afraid of them."

"Oh, dear. That's no fun."

"She's the stepdaughter of my friend Chaz Roylance, another P.I. at the firm," Travis explained. "It might interest you to know she's Lacey Pomeroy's three-year-old daughter."

Melissa's eyes flickered. "My favorite former host of the *Stargazer Paranormal* show?"

"The very one. They got married at the beginning of the summer. That's why she went off the air. He was hired to find the person stalking her. I'll tell you their story sometime. When the guys and I plan the next party, you'll meet her."

"I can't wait!"

"She's awesome," Casey interjected. "She believes in flying saucers."

"I know," Melissa said. "So do I."

"You do?"

Before there was any more talk, the TV announcer moved on to the next story.

"Once again Utah is in the news. Due to a tip-off, federal agents have seized a marijuana plantation in the mountains above Kamas. They estimate the street value of the marijuana, known as Early Misty, is $40 million. Our helicopter news team has been on the scene since early morning as agents and police swept in to confiscate guns and equipment, and burn what these illegals have tended all summer with the hope of harvesting.

"If you recall, there was a seizure of marijuana on Boulder Mountain several years ago. Utah seems to be becoming a prime target of cartels who are having trouble smuggling drugs across the Mexican border. They've chosen to grow their crop here and then ship it to the Midwest. These workers were caught red-handed and arrested on sight.

"It's determined they're from Colombia. They've labored hard all season to produce this huge crop, but sometimes hard work is not rewarded—as they've found out today. In this case, the Feds also captured a Colombian who's been on the FBI's Most Wanted list for close to two years. These mug shots identify him as Luis Manuel Carvelo, a notorious escaped convict now in custody after being wanted in Arizona for the deaths of six people."

Melissa's gasp reverberated through the kitchen. Travis saw her grow pale as she stared at him in disbelief. "That's the vile man at Grampy's!"

Travis walked over to turn off the TV. "He had a rap sheet as long as your arm."

"I can't believe it. How did he get hired?"

"He cut and bleached his hair. Using one of his aliases, he passed himself off as a former waiter from California, bilingual in Spanish, who moved to Kamas. He's been living in a camper parked in the garage of those people you told me about who vacation at Lake Tahoe."

"*That's* why you were asking me about them."

Travis nodded. "That camper was one of the vehicles used to transport the marijuana. He probably drove to your cabin many times. The tires on the vehicle matched the tracks outside your place. The whole thing was an elaborate setup, planned months ahead of its execution. Your cabin was closest to the area and made the perfect hangout."

Melissa shivered before getting to her feet. "All those awful men were living in my family's cabin."

"But they're gone now, huh, Daddy?"

Overjoyed that the danger to her was over, Travis reached for his son and lifted him in the air. "They sure are."

Melissa's eyes had filled with tears. "It's all because of you." Her voice shook. "You single-handedly took down a dangerous drug cartel. That criminal would still be out there, killing other people, if it weren't for you. I don't even know where to begin to thank you and your backup crew. My parents and I will always be indebted to you. I've got to call them right now!"

"Go ahead. We'll keep eating."

She dashed from the kitchen to get her phone. By the time they were finishing their lasagna, she reappeared. He could tell she'd been crying happy tears. "My parents want to talk to you." She handed him the phone.

For the next few minutes Travis explained to them what had transpired. They couldn't have been more grateful.

"When things have settled down," her father said, "we'd like to give a party to honor you and all the people at Lufka's who had any part in this. You've rid Kamas of a terrible menace. I guess you know by now this means more to us, and to our daughter, than words can say."

Travis *did* know. He had evidence of it in numerous ways. "She was a big help, Mr. Roberts. And, I might add, a very courageous woman, to keep going up there with me."

Her dad chuckled. "That cabin is special to her. We'll talk to her later and find a time when it's convenient for you to come to our house for an evening with the family, and of course, bring your son. She says he's a delightful young man. We're glad to hear his broken leg is all healed."

"Me, too."

"See you soon. Good night, Mr. Stillman."

Travis clicked off and handed the phone to Melissa who, along with Casey, was playing tug-of-war with one of the dog's toys. "Okay, everybody. What are we going to do after we clean up the kitchen?" Travis had no intention of letting this evening end.

"Can we go up to the cabin and have a sleepover tonight?"

Trust his son to come up with the perfect answer. "That's up to Melissa." Travis's gaze swerved to hers. "Have you had enough of the Stillman family?"

She hugged her arms to her waist in what he'd come to recognize as a nervous gesture. "I don't know what you're talking about. I was just thinking how exhausted you must be. Too tired to drive to Kamas again after all you've been through."

He put an arm around his son. "We love it up there, don't we, bud?"

"Yup."

"Well, if it's what you'd really like to do, then of course it's what I want more than anything."

Casey ran over and hugged her. "I'll have to drive to the town house first and get some more clothes and fresh bedding," she said, after hugging him back. "All the bedding up there needs to be thrown out. I don't want any reminders of what happened up there."

"I don't blame you. We'll clean up here, then head

for your condo and go up in my truck. On the way we'll buy a couple of bundles of wood, so we can make a fire tonight."

Casey gazed up at him in excitement. "Can we roast marshmallows?"

"In the house?" Travis replied.

"It'll be fine," Melissa assured him. "Our family does it all the time. After we get up there, we'll whittle some long sticks."

"Daddy has a really sharp knife."

"Great!" Her eyes flew to Travis. "Then we're set. When you buy the wood, pick up marshmallows and popcorn, too."

His son's shriek of happiness filled the house.

TWILIGHT WAS TURNING INTO darkness as they reached the cabin. Melissa had to pinch herself to believe they could drive right up to it in the truck without fear that someone was in there or was watching them from the forest.

While she opened the front door and turned on the generator so they could have lights, Casey helped his father bring in the groceries and wood. Dexter ran around sniffing in all the corners, while Travis went outside once more for their overnight bags. Melissa carried in the bedding she'd brought from her condo.

"Will you sleep with me again tonight?" Casey asked her.

Before Melissa could answer, Travis said, "You and I, bud, are going to sleep downstairs in one of the bedrooms. We'll let Melissa decide which one."

She flicked him a glance. "How about the one with

the big family picture on the wall? That bed is more comfortable. While you guys get the fire going, I'll put clean sheets and quilts on the beds we'll use tonight." The thought of those awful men using the bedrooms made her sick. While she was at it, she would give the bathrooms another scrubbing.

Their various jobs kept them busy. "Robin Hood had nothing on you," she said as Travis came in with three long, straight sticks, each with a point.

His wide smile caused her toes to curl. "Anything for you, my lady."

Once she'd microwaved the popcorn and poured it into a bowl, she put it and the bag of marshmallows in Casey's lap. He'd changed into his pajamas and was sitting in the middle of the couch, watching the flames. Dexter had jumped up and was nestled against his other side, inching his way toward the food.

After she'd lit two lanterns and turned off the generator, she brought napkins and planted herself on the couch next to him. "This is what I call cozy."

Travis's eyes when they met hers seemed to smolder, but maybe it was just a reflection of the fire. He asked Casey to hand him the marshmallows. "Don't feed any to Dexter or he'll get sick."

"I know. Can he have popcorn?"

"Maybe a couple."

Melissa watched with silent laughter as Casey fed the dog one piece of popcorn at a time, half hiding it under his leg.

Travis put a marshmallow on the end of a stick. "How do like yours cooked, Melissa?"

"Charred."

"That's funny. So do I."

"Yeah, black on the outside and gooey on the inside."

His deep chuckle seemed to rumble through her body. They'd probably have stomachaches in the morning, but she didn't care as she popped a third one in her mouth. Tonight wasn't like any other.

She was in love. Madly in love with a fabulous man.

As for his son, she loved him so much, she could almost believe she'd given birth to him.

The night wore on and the fire started to die down. Casey grew less talkative and eventually fell asleep against her shoulder. It had been a big day. Travis got to his feet with the stealth of a panther and carefully lifted the boy from the couch.

"Don't go away," he whispered to Melissa before carrying his son to the bedroom. As if she would go anywhere. His words acted like an electrical charge, igniting every part of her. Dexter jumped down and followed him.

Travis, without Dexter, returned in minutes. The look of desire he gave her couldn't be mistaken for anything else. She heard his sharp intake of breath before he got to the couch and followed her down with his body, pressing her against the cushions.

"Melissa," he cried urgently. "I need you tonight. Hold me. Kiss me."

He was actually trembling. In wonder, she wrapped her arms around him and let go of every inhibition, needing his kiss more than she needed air. She felt his fingers work their way into her hair. His touch brought exquisite pleasure.

Tonight she had the feeling he wanted *her.* That he was kissing *her,* not his deceased wife. Melissa didn't know how she knew. Maybe the talk with his sister had helped her turn a corner. All she knew was that this felt right and they were on fire for each other.

"If anything had happened to you…" he whispered against her throat. "The thought of him touching you…"

She cupped his face with her hands. "Him? Who are you talking about?"

He made a self-deprecating sound. "No one." He kissed her lips. "Forget what I said." Once again he crushed her mouth with his, thrilling her. But she couldn't get what he'd said out of her mind.

"Travis, what did you mean? You know I haven't been seeing another man."

A heavy sigh escaped his throat before he lifted his head. "One of the Colombians had been watching you. He talked about you. After Jose translated what was on the listening device, that was it. I couldn't let you come up here again until they were captured."

She wound her arms around his neck. "It was that predator at Grampy's, wasn't it?"

"It doesn't matter. He's been arrested. I can't believe I spoke my fears out loud." Travis buried his face in her hair.

Melissa could believe it. "You've just come off the case. It's only natural. Did you help with the actual arrests?"

"Yes. One of them led me on a wild chase and almost escaped."

She hugged him harder. "I can't comprehend hand-to-hand combat. You're made of sterner stuff than most men. I can't thank you enough for protecting me. To be that brave… As Casey always tells me, you're awesome." Melissa had run out of adjectives, and pressed her mouth to his, needing to show him how she felt.

Travis's hunger matched hers, but she was aware there was something troubling him deep down. As far as she knew, he'd still had no word of his wife's killer. But she didn't want to bring that up now. This had been the most heavenly night she'd ever known.

His mouth roved over her face, her throat, and he moaned. She gave an answering moan—she couldn't seem to get close enough to him, either. Suddenly she felt a shudder rack his powerful body. He levered himself away and got to his feet, putting distance between them. She was reeling. To be so passionately enthralled, and then for it to stop…

"What's wrong, Travis?"

He stared at her so strangely. "*This* is wrong. Several hours ago your parents thanked me for making the cabin safe for you. So what do I do? I bring you up here and ravage you, with my son in the next room."

"It's what I wanted, too. So tell me what really happened just now."

Travis had a habit of rubbing the back of his neck when he was trying to come up with an explanation he thought she could handle. But their relationship had gotten past that stage. "I could feel myself losing control," he said. "When I heard you moan, I remembered what you told me about your ex-husband."

She blinked. "That moan you heard was sheer ecstasy, not terror."

"How can I believe you? The last thing I want to do is make a fatal mistake with you and have you think I've suddenly turned into Mr. Hyde."

The bleak look on his face shattered her. She got to her feet. "Travis, he was a sick man. I've had enough therapy and have been with enough men since my divorce to realize Russ was one of a small few. When I met you, you were so in control there've been times when it's driven me crazy. You're the heroic Texas Ranger around everyone else, but when you're with me, I *want* you to be out of control."

"I want to believe you, but—"

"But what?" she interrupted. "Could this be a smoke screen for what's really going on here?"

His eyes narrowed to dark slits. "What do you mean?"

Sharp, stabbing pain took over. "I think you know. Ironic, isn't it? I can't get far enough away from the memory of my spouse. But you can't get close enough to yours. For a little while tonight you tried to forget, but before we got past the point of no return, you couldn't be tempted, because I wasn't Valerie.

"I'm not blaming you. How could I? She was the love of your life and hasn't been gone that long. It's a fact, and no skirting around the issue is going to change it."

"You're more wrong than you know." His voice sounded as if it came from a deep cavern.

"No. You grew up under a code of honor and couldn't forsake it if you tried. Tonight you proved it by not using me, by not pretending to feel something you couldn't feel. You're a noble soul, Travis. Believe me when I tell you that you're the finest man I've ever known. One day you'll get the reward you deserve simply for being *fantastic you*." She started for the wooden staircase.

"Melissa…"

She paused at the bottom and turned to him. "When you take me home tomorrow, I want it to be for the last time. I know it will be hard on Casey for a little while, but he'll get over it because he has you for a father. You'll know what to say to comfort him. Let's end it now so Casey won't realize what's happening when you drop me off tomorrow. Goodbye, Travis. Thank you for everything. God bless the two of you."

Chapter Ten

"How come you're not eating?"

Travis looked at Mitch. "I'm not hungry."

"That's what you said when we met here last week," Chaz reminded him.

The Cowboy Grub was their favorite hangout for breakfast, but meeting with his friends this morning had been a mistake. Since the marijuana bust a week ago, Travis had taken on and solved two new cases to keep busy, but his turmoil had reached a level where he could no longer function. The guys didn't deserve to see him like this.

"Is Casey still in as bad a shape as you?"

"Afraid so. He blames me and won't talk to me unless he has to."

"I understand his frustration." Mitch was a straight shooter. "Maybe you need to break down and tell us why you're really staying away from her. If you don't talk to somebody about this soon, you're going to crack."

Chaz nodded. "We'd like to help."

Travis rubbed his eyes, then stared at both of them. "Melissa suffered trauma in her marriage, and then suffered it again when her cabin was invaded. She doesn't need to get any more involved with me when we know Valerie's killer is still out there somewhere, looking for me."

"Chances are the Feds will catch up with him and he'll be locked away soon."

"True, Mitch," Travis replied. "And to Melissa's credit, she never brought it up after the first time I told her, but it isn't something you forget. Valerie hated my job as a Ranger. Melissa probably hates the work I do now."

"I hear you," Mitch said in a solemn tone. "When I asked Heidi to marry me, I have to admit I was relieved that the killer who'd tried to take me out back in Florida was finally in custody. But I wouldn't have let it stop me from being with her. Not unless she'd pulled away from me because of it."

Chaz eyed Travis with compassion. "I made a certain promise after I got out of the SEALs, but as we all know, in our business sometimes things go wrong despite our best efforts. I thought I'd lost Lacey because the stalker turned out to be her sister, but after she was arrested, Lacey found me while I was on vacation, and convinced me she was thankful for the work I did. In the end, she said it helped her sister get therapy, and it brought us together.

"As I see it, you need to go to Melissa. After you've told her the thing you're most worried about, let *her* decide if she wants to continue the relationship."

"If you stay away from her, you could be making the biggest mistake of your life," Mitch warned.

They were right.

Having made up his mind, Travis pushed himself away from the table and got to his feet. "I've got to talk to her. Thanks for being here for me."

"You've been there plenty for us."

Within a few minutes Travis was in his truck and on the way to her clinic. He decided not to phone. He couldn't risk her not calling him back. She'd told him Fridays were her busiest days, but he didn't care. He'd wait there until her lunch hour if he had to, so they could talk.

At nine-thirty he walked through the doors and headed straight for her office. To his frustration it was locked. He went to the exercise room, but she wasn't in there. Without hesitation he approached the secretary at the front desk. They recognized each other and nodded.

"Hi. I'm looking for Ms. Dalton."

"I'm afraid she won't be coming in today. She called in last evening and said she wasn't feeling well. But I'm sure she'll be back on Monday. If you're here to make an appointment for Casey, I'll schedule it in her calendar now."

"No, this is personal. If by any chance she should phone the clinic, will you ask her to call me pronto? She has my number."

"Of course."

Travis hurried outside. When he'd driven to the clinic, he'd been so anxious to see her, he hadn't been looking for her Jeep. Now that he glanced around, he realized it was nowhere in sight. He got back in the truck and took the route she normally drove to her town house. On the way he phoned her, but all he got was her voice mail. He asked her to call him.

When he drove up in front of the condo, one glance revealed her Jeep wasn't there, either. Maybe she'd gone to the pharmacy for some medicine. He knew which one and took off. The parking lot was only semifull. There was no Jeep anywhere.

Maybe she'd gone to her parents' or her brother's house. Travis phoned both numbers on the off chance she'd sought them out because she didn't feel well and wanted their company. Again he was met with voice mails. He left messages for them to contact him if they knew where he could reach Melissa.

His mind turned over other possibilities. She might have gone to the cabin after work last evening, and started feeling sick there. Since it was her favorite place, she'd probably decided to stay up there the whole weekend. Maybe she'd picked up a bug. Children coming in and out of the clinic carried germs and could have infected her.

The worrisome thought that she might be really sick and too weak to drive back down the canyon galvanized him into action. He took off for Kamas, breaking the speed limit all the way up. En route, he phoned Deana and asked her to pick up Casey after school. If he couldn't get back tonight, then she was to take him over to Pat's house for the night. It was time he and Melissa had a heart-to-heart.

AFTER ANOTHER RESTLESS NIGHT, Melissa got up determined to get some artwork done. But the creative juices weren't flowing and hadn't been since she'd said good-bye to Travis. Without bothering to dress, she stayed in her gray sweats and went downstairs in her zip-up slippers with her art supplies.

The generator was still on from last night. She fixed herself some instant coffee in the microwave, then turned off the switch. Silence reigned once more, the way it was supposed to in the forest. She opened the back door to a beautiful fall morning. Utah truly was a land of sunny skies.

Once she'd finished her drink, she put her folding chair outside the back door and set up her easel. She'd brought her big art pad down, along with her acrylics. Being up here, instead of at work at the clinic, should have made her feel guilty. But Melissa had been feeling ill all week and knew she couldn't have made it through today's heavy schedule.

She didn't know how to fix her broken heart.

Travis…

Tears rolled down her cheeks. Without realizing it, she began doing a sketch of his well-shaped head. He was a man in his prime, with lines of experience and character etched into his face. A beyond-gorgeous jaw, a wide mouth that could harden or soften, depending on his mood…

His deep-set blue eyes gleamed with intelligence. His ears and nose were in perfect proportion to his other features. His hair was a dark, rich chestnut. And the way he was put together left every other man she'd known out of the competition.

Her love for him poured out on the paper. She didn't

need to see him in person; he was inscribed on her mind and heart for all time. Anything he wore suited him, but she had to admit she loved the hunter-green shirt he'd worn to the clinic with Casey, a button-down with a collar. She drew it in.

After studying the finished product for a minute, she signed and dated it. Beneath her signature she wrote "My Superhero." This portrait and the one she'd done of Casey were her most prized possessions.

It felt good to spill her emotions onto paper. Once she went back in the cabin and got dressed, she would take a hike with some of her supplies and see if she could find that elk. So noble and majestic. She saw Travis's spirit like that.

She closed her art pad. As she started to gather everything up, someone shoved her to the ground and covered her mouth and nose from behind, cutting off her air. She felt a hard chest as a man slammed down on top of her. In shock, she fought and twisted, managing to bite the grubby hand mashing her face. Blood spurted everywhere.

She heard a string of invectives, but he never let go. There was a ripping sound before he started wrapping her mouth with duct tape. After he got off her and set her on her feet, he turned her around. She made a huge scratch down the side of his acne-pocked cheek before he tied her hands in front of her with a rope.

Melissa's captor was no taller than she was, but he was heavyset and strong as a bull. He put one of his legs between hers so she couldn't move. Blood was now dripping from his face and spattering everywhere.

She'd heard nothing before he'd sneaked up behind her. Her legs shook at the possibility of him having spent the night in the cabin with her, waiting for this opportunity. He had to be one of the illegals who'd escaped the sting operation. She could moan all she wanted for help, but the tape had silenced her, and she was feeling claustrophobic.

"Cooperate with me," he said at last, "and you might live long enough to watch me shoot your boyfriend between the eyes. But I won't do that until he sees you're with me. We'll wait for him to come. After he's dead, I plan to have some fun with you before I finish you off."

This lowlife wasn't a Colombian. In fact, he had a Southern drawl. This monster was a white guy covered in tattoos. About her height, he had stringy brown hair that hung in his face. Each time he tossed his head back, it fell over his brows again.

The second she divined the truth of his origins, he said, "Didn't he tell you about me? I'm sure he did. I'm Danny, the only survivor of the McClusky brothers. We were famous down in Texas. I'm not including Fred, of course. He died a long time ago, when we went swimming and he accidentally drowned. That left Donny and Davey."

Her soul screamed in terror. *This lunatic is Valerie's killer!* Somehow he'd tracked Travis down. Much as Melissa wanted this to be a nightmare, it wasn't.

"We were doing great on our own until some rats squealed on us and we had to kill them. From then on, everything went wrong, and that damn Texas Ranger came after us."

Her captor started leading her into the forest by the rope binding her hands. There was no possibility of getting away from him. He was out of shape and was forced to stop every few steps to take deep breaths, but he continued to pull her through the undergrowth to the top of the ridge behind the cabin.

Where his plaid shirt separated from his pants, she saw another repulsive tattoo. Wanting to take advantage of the early morning light, she hadn't eaten breakfast. That was good, because she would have thrown up.

To her horror, he found two trees growing close together at the edge of a clearing, and spread-eagled her upright between them. Using more rope, he fastened her wrists and ankles so tightly they burned. He groped her on and off. When she tried to elude him, the ropes twisted into her skin. The pain was unbearable. She couldn't sit, bend or lie down.

"I wasn't going to let him put us in prison. But during our escape, Donny and Davey got mowed down by him without them knowing what hit them." While he was stringing her up, the man babbled and bawled like a baby. Then he suddenly turned around with a murderous gleam in his eyes.

"I couldn't let that go, now could I? Not Danny Mc-Clusky. So I took my time before I picked off your Ranger's wife so he'd get the message. Then I figured that still wasn't good enough. No siree. The Bible says 'an eye for an eye.' He took two of my family, so I decided to take two of his to make things fair. Don't you see?"

Yes. Melissa saw it only too clearly. But his plan was

faulty. When Travis didn't show up, this madman would eventually get tired of waiting, and come up with another plan. At that point, she would probably be dead. But if by some miracle she was still breathing, she might be able to get away from him.

She had to pray that, with a week having gone by already, Travis had decided not to try to see her again. Surely after this long he'd come to the conclusion that a permanent parting was best for all of them.

What bitter irony! All this week she'd been praying he'd call or come to the clinic, because he couldn't live without her and wanted to convince her of that. She'd lain awake all last night debating whether to call *him*. Life without him was no life at all. While she'd been finishing her portrait of Travis earlier, she'd made up her mind that when she got back to Salt Lake, she'd phone him and ask him to come to her condo so they could really talk.

Incredibly, this killer had kidnapped her at the very moment she'd been planning what she would say to Travis. Now there was no second chance to blurt out her love for him. This monster had the upper hand and would be watching for him if he did come up here looking for her. There'd be no way to warn him except to moan loudly enough that he might hear her. But by then it would be too late.

"I've been looking for over a year. He thought he could escape me, but it just goes to show he isn't as smart as he thinks he is. I have friends who helped me track him down. I found him, all right. And what do you know—he has a kid and a girlfriend."

This was a scene right out of a bad movie.

He was criminally insane and would carry out his plan as surely as the sun went down at night.

"I'm going to keep you tied up right here until he comes for you. I figure if I take you and him out together, that leaves the kid. I'll kill him later."

Oh, my darling Casey!

"Ranger boy sure knows how to pick 'em."

A cold layer of sweat enveloped her body as Danny McCluskey ran his hands over her. She gathered her strength and head-butted him, the impact causing more blood to trickle down his face and chin. She was bleeding, too, but it had been worth it.

With such a short fuse at this point, he was angered by everything. He kept looking around like a crazed animal, obviously expecting someone would come.

She thought again of her last night here at the cabin with Travis. She'd been so afraid he still wanted Valerie that she'd ended it with him. And because she knew her family's plans, Melissa realized no one would be coming up to Kamas this weekend.

For the first time in her life, she had a conviction she was going to die. But not without a fight!

After what seemed like hours of being strung up in this condition, she discovered her eyes staring at the ground cover. Her head drooped, feeling as if it weighed a hundred pounds. If only she could have some water, but there was no way he was going to untape her mouth. Her arms had gone numb and she found it hard to breathe.

It could be days that he left her out here. Or he might

decide to rape and shoot her before he went back to Salt Lake to hunt down Travis and Casey. This maniac would have no qualms about doing something horrible to a boy she loved like her own son. She needed to save them both, but how?

RELIEF SURGED THROUGH Travis when he drove up the road from town and saw her Jeep parked at the cabin. He jumped from the cab and raced to the front door.

"Melissa?" He started knocking. When she didn't answer, he knocked again and waited. He rang her phone once more. No answer. With the sun shining overhead, she might be out in back sketching or painting, even if she didn't feel well.

"Melissa?" he called as he walked toward the rear of the cabin. The last thing he wanted to do was frighten her. "It's Travis! If you can hear me, answer me!" The second he rounded the corner his gut twisted, squeezing the breath out of him.

Not only was the back door open, but there were signs of a struggle. The lawn chair she used had been tipped over and dented. Her acrylic paint tubes were scattered in every direction. He stooped to pick up her art pad, lying on top of an easel that appeared broken.

His heart jumped in terror when he saw blood spatters on the pad.

A few feet away he saw her cell phone, open. He checked her last outgoing call. It had been to her parents at five o'clock yesterday evening. Whoever had surprised her had abducted her too fast for her to call for help.

If she was inside, he had to find out. His training in law enforcement had prepared him for this, but not when the victim was the woman he was crazy in love with.

He hadn't seen Valerie when she was shot. His boss had been the one to tell him. This was different. If he found Melissa lying in there...

Saying a prayer, he went inside. A thorough search turned up nothing. That meant there was a chance she was still alive.

He phoned the firm on his own cell. "Roman?" Travis was in such a rage over the fiend who'd done this, he could hardly manage words. "I'm at Melissa's cabin. Looks like she's been abducted. One of the Colombians must have escaped the net while we were rounding them up a week ago, and has been hiding out. Maybe she caught him using the cabin while she was painting. There's evidence she fought him.

"I'm going after her right now. If this scum thinks he's being followed, there's no telling what he'll do to Melissa. He has plans for her, or he would have killed her on the spot."

"What can I do?" Roman asked.

"Send up Jose and Lon. Tell them to drive to the fire-break road where the marijuana was loaded." There was no doubt in Travis's mind the kidnapper had dragged her to the area where he'd been working most of the summer. "They'll know where to head from there. I'll phone them in a little while."

"I'm on it and will have a helicopter standing by," Roman said. "Go get him."

Travis hurried to his truck. He pulled out his heat-seeking goggles and handgun from his backpack. After putting the weapon in his leg holster, he retrieved his rifle from the locker in the back of the truck. Fully equipped, Travis started through the forest on a run.

He had to find her—find her in time...

Forty-five minutes later he got a call from Jose. The guys were rushing to the harvest site and would stay in touch. He hung up and kept moving until his thermal goggles picked up an image he hadn't expected to see until he reached his destination.

His heart slammed against his ribs when he saw Melissa strung out between two trees, her head down. A man armed with a rifle emerged from the pines behind her. Travis got down on the ground behind a log. Using it as a prop for his rifle, he took aim at the man's shoulder and pulled the trigger.

The wounded man fell not two feet from Melissa. His rifle landed just out of his reach. He howled from where he lay, spewing venom as Travis ran toward Melissa.

In the next instant he was cutting the ropes off her and gently laying her unconscious form on the ground. He removed the tape from across her mouth, careful not to take any skin with it. He felt for her pulse and rejoiced when he found one. It was weak, but it was there.

Then he pulled out his cell to call Roman. "The kidnapper has been incapacitated. I've got Melissa, but she's unconscious and needs medical attention. Send a helicopter to the clearing where the marijuana was burned. Here are the coordinates. Tell Jose and Lon."

Still hunkered down beside Melissa, Travis pulled a

bottle of water from his pocket and talked to her while he sprinkled droplets on her face in an effort to revive her. "Come on, sweetheart, be alive for me and Casey."

He could hear the chopper now. Suddenly Lon and Jose were on the scene, followed by police. In another minute a medical team was running forward with a stretcher.

Once she was safely strapped on, Travis followed and climbed into the helicopter with her. The blades were still rotating. Within seconds, the craft took off and the team began the process of hooking her up to an IV. After taking her vital signs, they put an oxygen mask over her face.

"Do you think she will be okay?" Travis asked.

"Give her time. She's been through a rough ordeal. We heard she'd been spread-eagled. With her arms extended that tight, and above her heart, she's had a hard time breathing. The oxygen will help her. Don't worry. We'll be at University Hospital in a few minutes."

One of the medics told Travis he looked pale, and suggested he sit down, but he couldn't leave her. He looked at her wrists and ankles. The ropes had made angry-looking red rings around them.

It was because of him that Melissa was on the verge of losing her life. He should have made certain they'd caught every illegal operating up there. Maybe since Valerie's death, he'd lost his edge and should get out of law enforcement altogether. He had to be slipping if one of those Colombians had eluded capture. All week the trash had probably stayed at her cabin at night, waiting for her to show up.

By the time they reached the hospital, she still hadn't gained consciousness. Travis's pain was unbearable as he watched them wheel her into Emergency.

Roman met him as he walked through the doors behind the stretcher. "She might not make it," Travis rasped.

"She was alive when you found her. Don't lose hope now."

"I'm no good anymore, Roman. This is my fault. I wasn't thorough enough during the sting. One got away, and now Melissa's life is on the line because of my mistake."

Roman grabbed his shoulders. "What are you talking about? Don't you know it was Danny McClusky who kidnapped her?"

"What?" Travis's mind reeled.

Chaz spoke up behind him. "He tracked you here, but received the surprise of his life when you got him with your rifle."

"It's true," Mitch interjected. "Your wife's death has been avenged in a miraculous way. As I see it, you have smooth sailing from here on out."

Travis grimaced. "Not if Melissa doesn't make it. She must wish she'd never met me."

"You know better than that. Let's go see how she's doing."

The four of them walked toward the cubicle, but were told to wait until the doctors had finished their examination. Travis buried his face in his hands. The waiting felt like an eternity.

"Travis?"

He looked up to see Jose and Lon, who'd just come in on the other helicopter. Lon was carrying her bloodied sketch pad. "We thought you might like to see what's inside." He flipped it open and Travis found himself looking at his own image. He was staggered by Melissa's talent. And the words at the bottom said it all.

Roman's eyes gleamed. "It's a very good likeness of you, comrade. I think we should hang it in the office."

"Notice the date." Chaz was smiling.

It had been this morning.

Tears prickled Travis's eyelids. "If it hadn't been for you guys urging me to talk to her…"

"You'd have gone to find her, anyway. You were a mess without her," Mitch said.

Chaz nodded. "You were."

Suddenly, a doctor stepped from behind the curtain. "Is one of you Travis? The patient's asking for him."

Travis felt half a dozen slaps on his back before he rushed into the cubicle.

She was bruised and banged up. They'd cleaned her forehead and had put a butterfly tape over the cut. She was hooked up to oxygen, as well as an IV, but it didn't matter because her eyes were open. And she was the most beautiful sight he'd ever seen.

Her poor mouth was covered in blisters, and he lowered his head and kissed her cheek. When he met her gaze, his eyes filled with tears.

"I prayed you'd c-come," Melissa said, her voice weak. "Then I prayed you w-wouldn't because he was waiting for you. He threatened to kill C-Casey." Tears gushed from her eyes and down her temples to the sheet. "Is Casey all right? Does he know anything?"

"He's fine," Travis whispered "And no, he knows nothing about this."

"Don't ever let him know. I want him to always love the cabin."

"It will be our secret."

The doctor pulled the curtain aside. "I'm sorry to disturb you, but we're taking her upstairs to a private room. She's been given a sedative. You can come, but she needs to rest now."

"Understood."

"Don't l-leave me, Travis."

"I won't, I swear."

As he left the cubicle, an older couple rushed forward. "I'm Melissa's mother. We're so grateful to you for saving our daughter's life, you'll never know." She hugged him with surprising strength.

Over her head Melissa's father was smiling through tears.

"They're taking her up to a private room," Travis said. "I promised I wouldn't leave her, but I need to call my son. Then I'll join you."

"Go right ahead. We'll see you upstairs."

When he walked outside the emergency room doors to make the call, he announced to his waiting friends, "She's going to be fine."

"That's all we wanted to hear."

Lon handed him the art pad. "I think you'll want to hold on to this. I've got the rest of your stuff and will bring it to the office. A couple of police officers are bringing the truck and Jeep down from the cabin. I told them to drive both to Melissa's house so your son won't be alarmed."

"You think of everything."

Lon smiled. "I'm a father, too."

After everyone left in Roman's big van, Travis phoned Pat.

"Casey's been hoping you'd call," his sister said. "Here he is."

"Dad?"

"Hi, bud. How was school today?"

"It was okay. When are you coming home?"

"Well, I have a date with Melissa tonight."

"You do?" he half squealed in joy.

"Yeah. The problem is, I might get home late."

"Is that 'cuz you're going to kiss and stuff?"

"What makes you think that?" Travis teased.

"I saw you kissing, and Zack told me that's what his parents do all the time."

Travis chuckled. "Will it be okay if you don't see me until tomorrow morning?"

"Yeah. Do you think Melissa will come with you?"

"We'll see."

"You always say that!"

"I know. I love you, Casey." His voice shook. "See you in the morning."

Chapter Eleven

Melissa awakened when the nurse came into her room at 7:00 a.m. on her rounds. That's when she saw Travis seated on a chair next to her bed, studying one of the drawings in her art pad. He looked drained and exhausted. And never more attractive.

The nurse took her vitals and checked the IV. "At this rate you'll be able to go home today." She took the IV out of her arm. "Are you hungry for more than juice?"

"Yes. I'd love some toast."

"I'll bring you some. After breakfast you can get up and shower."

"That sounds heavenly." The nurse's visit reminded Melissa she must look awful.

"The doctor will be in later to check on you."

"Thank you."

Melissa was feeling well enough not to like the way the pretty nurse smiled at Travis before she left the room. Melissa wanted Travis out of the line of fire from all the females working here.

Finally they were alone.

"Hi," she said to this incredible man who'd saved her life.

His warm gaze traveled over her. "How are you feeling?"

"I can't wait to get out of here."

"Ah. If that's true, then it means you're well enough to kiss."

Her pulse raced when he got up and moved close. "You might not like the taste of the salve they put on my lips."

"Don't you know by now that won't stop me?"

"Oh, Travis…" He leaned over and kissed her gently. She didn't want gentle, and flung her arms around his neck to pull him closer. "I love you, I love you. If you don't feel the same way, it doesn't matter."

"But I *do* feel the same way. If you weren't still in the hospital, I'd show you just how much I love you, darlin'. Only you and nobody else."

Though her lips were still tender, she kissed him with all she had. "Yesterday I was afraid I'd never see you again," she said long moments later. "I was a fool to end things with you. It wasn't what I wanted. All week I wanted to call you and tell you I was wrong."

"You don't even *want* to know about the week I had without you." He kissed her neck and throat.

"I'm to blame. You see, I'm a very spoiled girl. But I've repented for wishing to be the first and only love in your life. When I was tied with those ropes, I realized how lucky I was to be the current woman in your life."

Travis raised his head. Even in the dim light, his eyes blazed with fire. "Not only current, but the only one for the rest of our lives."

Her eyes filled. "You mean…"

"I'm asking you to marry me. But before you answer me, I need to ask you something else, and you have to be honest with me."

"Oh, for heaven's sake! I fell in love with a Texas Ranger. That's what you'll always be to me, and I wouldn't want you any other way. As your oh-so-wise sister said to me recently, there are no guarantees in this life. Let's agree to love each other and stop worrying about what might happen. Frankly, I'm sick of it."

A chuckle escaped his throat before he worked an arm beneath her head so he could give her the deep kind of kiss she was aching for. When he finally relinquished her mouth, she whispered, "I'll marry you whenever it can be arranged, but before this conversation goes any further, *I* need an answer to a very important question."

"This wouldn't have anything to do with children, would it? Because if it does, you need to know I want more than one. Valerie was afraid to have more for fear—"

Melissa put a finger to his lips. "Say no more. I've always wanted a family of three or four children, as long as it was with the right man. We've already got our first with Casey. Besides you, he's the light of my life. But there's a cabin up in Kamas with enough bedrooms to house a new generation."

The two of them were laughing when the doctor popped in. "That's a happy sound I hear." He eyed Travis. "If you'll step out for a minute."

"Of course."

When Melissa was alone with the doctor, she said, "If

my heart rate is up, it's because of him. He just asked me to marry him."

The doctor finished checking her over. "I take it you said yes?"

"Oh, yes."

The man smiled. "Under the circumstances, I'll sign you out to go home, but go easy for a few days. Have your regular doctor check the cut on your forehead in a week. If that bandage did its job, there shouldn't be a scar. If there is, you can check with a plastic surgeon. Stay hydrated."

"I will. Thank you."

Melissa couldn't wait to see Casey's reaction to their news.

"It's ELEVEN O'CLOCK, Dad. How come it took you so long to pick me up?"

Travis glanced in the rearview mirror at his son and Dexter before he started the truck. "Melissa bumped her forehead getting out of the Jeep. I had to take her to the doctor to get a bandage put on it."

His eyes rounded. "Did she need stitches?"

"Nope. She just has a little headache."

"Oh."

That was the story they felt would go down best with Casey. After going to Melissa's town house in a taxi, he'd picked up his truck and driven back to the hospital to take her home.

"Where are we going?"

"To the grocery store."

"Can Melissa come to our house after?"

"I thought we'd go over to her condo."

"I've never been in it before."

"That's because I've been doing a job for her at the cabin, Casey. When I'm working for a client, I don't generally go to their houses. But now that the case has been solved, she has invited us over, even Dexter."

"I bet she doesn't want me to come."

Travis hadn't been expecting a statement like that. "Of course she does. In fact, she asked me to bring you." He waited for a burst of excitement that didn't happen. "Hey, bud, what's wrong?"

"Nothing."

"I thought you loved her. I know she loves *you*."

"She just says that to be nice."

"She *is* nice, but I don't think she tells that to her other patients. Do you?"

"I don't know." The little boy sighed and looked out the window.

Travis couldn't get any more out of him during their trip to the store. When they pulled up in front of the town house, Casey got out of the backseat with Dexter and headed for her front door. Suddenly it opened.

"Hi, Casey!" That bright voice reminded Travis of those first moments at the clinic. "I'm so glad you're here. Come in!" Melissa stood there in jeans and a creamy, long-sleeved sweater that hid the rope burns on her wrists and ankles.

Amazing what makeup could do. She'd covered up the bruise on the side of her cheek where McClusky had shoved her to the ground. Somehow the lipstick she was wearing disguised the tender spots. Her hair had been freshly washed and left loose to swing against the sides of her neck. On the whole, she didn't look as if she'd been through the ordeal he'd witnessed yesterday.

But one thing was missing. He could tell she was waiting for Casey's hug. When it didn't happen, she darted Travis an anxious glance as he put the groceries on the kitchen counter at the other end of the living room.

An exuberant Dexter danced around her, but Travis couldn't say the same for his son who stared at the bandage. "Does your head hurt?"

"I took a painkiller and now I feel fine. Thanks for asking. You've never been in my house before, have you? It's really little. Would you like to take a tour?"

"Okay."

Melissa worked with children all the time. She was a master at not showing her surprise over his uncharacteristic behavior, and pretended he was delighted to be here.

While they walked around, Travis followed. On the living room walls she'd hung a grouping of large framed prints of Picasso and Matisse. Her contemporary furniture added the rest of the color. The place exuded warmth.

They went down the hall. She'd turned the smaller bedroom into an art studio. He could tell Casey was impressed, but the boy remained sober.

In her bedroom, small framed photographs of her family sat on the dresser. Casey studied everything, and was ready to walk out again when he blurted, "Hey, Dad, look!"

"Where?"

"Over the bed. Melissa painted *me!*"

In a twinkling, his whole demeanor changed.

Travis put his arm around Casey's shoulder and they moved closer to examine the good-size framed painting hanging over her bed. He could have sworn this hadn't been on the wall when he'd helped her into the house after leaving the hospital.

The picture filled him with wonder. It *was* Casey, but an older version, the way he might look around age twelve. Melissa had painted him riding an animal with three horns, a creative figment of her imagination. She'd shown him emerging from a prehistoric forest.

He wore animal skins on his lean body and a thong around his forehead, with his chestnut hair spilling over. One hand clutched a spear. His leg carried a jagged scar from thigh to the ankle. The sight of the young superhero brought tears to Travis's eyes.

"Do you like it?" she asked Casey. Travis heard the tremor in her voice.

"I love it! I didn't know you painted me."

"I did this after I first met you, but I've kept it a secret." The revelation thrilled and humbled Travis.

"How come?" Casey asked.

"Because I take care of children all the time, but I'm not supposed to love one of them so much, that I wished he were my son. I love you, Casey. I think I love you too much. That's why I didn't read a story to you the other night. I wanted to be your mommy, but I knew I wasn't, and I was afraid you'd see me cry."

He walked over and looked up at her with eyes more

brilliantly blue than Travis had ever seen them. "Do you want to be my new mom?"

Tears poured down her cheeks. "Yes. More than anything in the world."

Now came the hug. Casey almost crushed her. They clung for a long time.

"You know how you have that picture of your daddy above your bed because you love him?" she finally asked.

His son nodded.

"That's the same reason I have your picture above mine."

Casey's head whipped around. "Dad?"

"She loves you, Casey. Did you hear that?" His son literally glowed with happiness. "And do you know what's *really* amazing?"

"What?"

"She loves me, too."

"I already know that."

"How do you know?" His eyes met Melissa's while they waited for Casey to come out with something startling.

"'Cuz I've seen you kissing."

Travis laughed for sheer joy. "Well, there's one thing I bet you don't know."

"What?"

"I asked Melissa to marry me last night."

"I *knew* you were going to."

"You knew?" Melissa made a sound between a laugh and a cry.

"Yup. You said you were going on a date with her.

Zack said that after Mitch kissed Heidi on a date, they got married."

"Sheer deduction." Melissa grinned at Travis. "I'm not surprised. It looks like those two are so smart, they'll probably grow up to be P.I.s like their dads."

"Nope." Casey shook his head. "I'm going to be a Texas Ranger!"

Melissa embraced them both. "Your son has mighty big shoes to fill," she whispered against Travis's cheek. "Will you do me one more favor?"

He kissed her temple. "Anything."

"Please don't let me die of too much happiness yet. Our lives are just beginning."

Chapter Twelve

Outside the cabin windows, golden fall colors interspersed with green pines provided the backdrop for the wedding. Inside, the flowers on the stands by the fireplace and placed around the family room mimicked the tones nature had provided: elegant red roses, orange Asiatic lilies, bronze cushion spray and yellow Viking spray chrysanthemums mixed with greenery. Dark red tapered candles had been added to highlight the rustic setting.

Melissa knew how much Casey was looking forward to Halloween, so she and Travis had planned to get married the Saturday before.

They both wanted a small affair. Only family and close friends on either side, with Melissa's pastor officiating. Even so, a lot of cars lined the road into the cabin. Snow was forecast for the late evening, but she wasn't worried, because after the four o'clock ceremony, followed by a celebration, everyone would have time to get home before it started. Then she'd be alone with her husband, able to shower him with the love she felt for him. Just the thought made her pulse race.

Casey would be going back with his aunt Pat and her family. Later on, in the spring, Travis planned to take them on a week's honeymoon. For now, two nights away was probably as much as Casey could handle.

When they came back down from the cabin, they'd drive straight to Travis's home. They'd already moved her things in, and Melissa had arranged to sublet her town house. Everything had been done, except the ceremony to make them husband and wife.

"Melissa?" the pastor said. "If you and Travis will join me and hold hands…"

Travis, stunning in a tux, intertwined his fingers with hers before they moved to stand in front of the pastor. Melissa wore a cap-sleeved, knee-length, raw-silk dress in an eggshell color. She knew Travis liked her hair long, so she'd left it loose, and wore two roses behind one ear.

"Dearly beloved, we're gathered here in the heart of these mountains to join Melissa Jeremy Roberts and Travis Cederlof Stillman in holy matrimony. It was here they found their love, and so it's appropriate they seal their vows on this very spot.

"All of you here know the way the lives of these two have been fraught with difficult and dangerous obstacles. The fact that they've survived so beautifully shows not only the indomitable human spirit, but proves they've literally fulfilled that part of the vows where they take each other 'for worse.'"

He smiled. "What's left is the 'for better,' and then to go on loving each other, whether rich or poor, through sickness and health, to the end of your lives and be-yond. Travis, do you take this woman to be your wife?"

"I do," he said in his deep voice.

"Melissa? Do you take this man to be your husband?"

"With all my heart."

Travis squeezed her hand.

"Then by the power vested in me, I pronounce you husband and wife. What God has joined together, let no man put asunder. Casey?" He nodded at their son, who was standing by with a huge smile. "If you'll come forward with the rings…"

Melissa's eyes brimmed with unshed tears as the little boy, dressed in a tux like his father, and carry-ing the rings on a pillow, stepped forward. At that mo-ment she could see handsome Casey as a grown man, wearing a tux at his own wedding. One day she would paint him like that. But that time was years away yet, thank heaven!

Travis picked up the interlocking rings and slid them on her finger. Two blue-white diamonds sparkled up at her. He'd been extravagant, but he told her that one diamond represented his love. The other represented Casey's, and they came as a package deal.

With a less than steady hand, she took the gold band she'd picked out for him and put it on his ring finger. When she looked up, Travis pulled her into his arms. In front of everyone he kissed her with long-suppressed hunger before the pastor had time to say anything.

"We know how you feel, comrade," Travis's boss called out in his Russian accent, "but it's time to wind this up."

The onlookers laughed. After being congratulated, Melissa was engulfed with hugs and the party began.

Casey and Zack drank a lot of punch and worked their way through the crowd to her. Abby tagged along behind them. Melissa hugged all three of them before she picked up Casey in her arms and kissed him. "You're my boy now," she said, before lowering him to the floor.

"Yup."

"We'll be outside in front of your school on Monday to take you home. Are you going to be all right till then? You can always call us. We told your aunt."

"I know. Are you going to stay right here?"

"What do *you* think?" Travis had come back and engulfed them in his strong arms. "Melissa and I aren't going anywhere. This is our favorite place."

"Mine, too."

"Your aunt Pat and uncle Jerry are waving to us. It's started snowing. They want to get down the canyon before it piles up. I need another hug."

Casey hugged them both hard, but to his credit he didn't break down and cry. With Zack watching, he had too much pride.

"Call us when you get home, okay, bud?"

"Yup."

"We love you, sweetheart," Melissa said emotionally. With that, he ran through the cabin to the front door, where his aunt and uncle were waiting.

Pretty soon everyone was leaving. Her parents were the last to go. "I don't have to worry about you taking care of her." Melissa saw her dad's affection for Travis. Her parents were crazy about him. More hugs ensued before quiet reigned and they were finally alone.

When she heard Travis turn the lock of the front door, adrenaline began to flow through her body. Her breath caught as he turned to her. Those dark blue eyes were burning with desire for her.

Without saying a word, he walked around, blowing out the candles. Without the generator on, all they heard were the sizzles coming from the fire dying down in the fireplace. Only the fading light from the flames lit the room.

He slid his hand to her neck and they walked over to the window looking out on the forest behind the cabin. "Our first snowfall together. It's so beautiful, Travis."

"Not as beautiful as my wife." He unexpectedly picked her up as if she weighed nothing, and started for the staircase. "I wanted to do this the night we came up here so I could plant the cameras. Watching you climb the steps gave me ideas I shouldn't have been having."

She pressed a warm kiss to his mouth. "I had the same ideas, Travis, but no matter how hard it's been to wait, I'm glad we did. It makes this night unique in our lives."

He returned her kiss as he carried her over the threshold of her bedroom. "You're so precious to me, Melissa. I adore you. Love me tonight, darling. You have no idea how much I need you."

Who would ever have thought that helping each other out of their clothes could be such a breathtaking experience? Time and space had no meaning as they became lovers. They became one flesh, giving and taking pleasure throughout the night.

When morning came, and dazzling sunlight streamed in the window, reflecting off the snow, Melissa found herself nestled against his chest with their legs entwined. She lifted her head. With him asleep, she could feast her eyes on him all she wanted.

No woman could possibly feel the euphoria that enveloped her this morning. It was because no woman alive had been loved into oblivion by this particular Texas Ranger.

Unable to resist, she kissed him around his lips to tease him awake. When he responded by searching for her mouth, she kissed his jaw.

His eyes opened. He took a deep breath. "What are you trying to do to me, woman?"

"So you call me 'woman' now."

"That's right." He raised up and proceeded to crush her mouth with refined savagery. At last he raised his head. "And I'm your man."

"Yes," she said breathlessly.

Another hour passed before she was in any state to form a coherent sentence. "Darling? Could I ask you an important question?"

He gazed at her. "Sure, but what else could you want to know?"

"With the threat of that killer gone, would you like to move back to Fort Davis? There must be a part of you that misses the association with your coworkers. After all the phone calls from them and your former boss, plus the citation from the governor of Texas for meritorious service, don't you miss that life? Because if you do, I have no problem with us moving there.

"I can always find a job in my profession, and I can paint anywhere. The important thing is for you and Casey to be happy. I realize the P.I. job saved your sanity when you moved here, but there has to be a huge chunk of your life you still feel is missing."

He leaned over her, plunging his hand in her hair. "After what you just said, I love you more than ever. But you need to know that with Valerie's death, my days as a Ranger ended. I came here to start a new life and I've learned to love it. My new friends at Lufka's are the greatest. The work I do is just as challenging.

"As for Casey, he has family here. Because of that family, he fell off one of their horses, and the accident that followed ultimately brought us into the exciting world of Melissa Dalton. That was the day the whole world changed for the Stillman family." He cupped her face with his hands. "I don't want to change anything. I want my wife right where she is—in my heart and my bed."

She smiled. "That's all I needed to hear. I guess it will have to be up to Casey to continue the Texas Ranger tradition."

"Maybe. If it's what he really wants."

Melissa raised herself on one elbow. "I think we'd better call him and let him know that we're alive and fine. So far he's shown great restraint."

Travis's smile lit up her universe. "He has, hasn't he?"

"I love that boy. I hope we can give him a little brother or sister."

"After we phone him, I think we should do our best to make that happen."

"Oh, yes, please!"

* * * * *

REQUEST YOUR FREE BOOKS!
2 FREE NOVELS PLUS 2 FREE GIFTS!

◆ Harlequin®

American ★ Romance®

LOVE, HOME & HAPPINESS

YES! Please send me 2 FREE Harlequin® American Romance® novels and my 2 FREE gifts (gifts are worth about $10). After receiving them, if I don't wish to receive any more books, I can return the shipping statement marked "cancel." If I don't cancel, I will receive 4 brand-new novels every month and be billed just $4.49 per book in the U.S. or $5.24 per book in Canada. That's a saving of at least 14% off the cover price! It's quite a bargain! Shipping and handling is just 50¢ per book in the U.S. and 75¢ per book in Canada.* I understand that accepting the 2 free books and gifts places me under no obligation to buy anything. I can always return a shipment and cancel at any time. Even if I never buy another book, the two free books and gifts are mine to keep forever.

154/354 HDN FEP2

Name _____ (PLEASE PRINT)

Address _____ Apt. #

City _____ State/Prov. _____ Zip/Postal Code

Signature (if under 18, a parent or guardian must sign)

Mail to the **Reader Service:**
IN U.S.A.: P.O. Box 1867, Buffalo, NY 14240-1867
IN CANADA: P.O. Box 609, Fort Erie, Ontario L2A 5X3

Not valid for current subscribers to Harlequin American Romance books.

Want to try two free books from another line?
Call 1-800-873-8635 or visit www.ReaderService.com.

* Terms and prices subject to change without notice. Prices do not include applicable taxes. Sales tax applicable in N.Y. Canadian residents will be charged applicable taxes. Offer not valid in Quebec. This offer is limited to one order per household. All orders subject to credit approval. Credit or debit balances in a customer's account(s) may be offset by any other outstanding balance owed by or to the customer. Please allow 4 to 6 weeks for delivery. Offer available while quantities last.

Your Privacy—The Reader Service is committed to protecting your privacy. Our Privacy Policy is available online at www.ReaderService.com or upon request from the Reader Service.

We make a portion of our mailing list available to reputable third parties that offer products we believe may interest you. If you prefer that we not exchange your name with third parties, or if you wish to clarify or modify your communication preferences, please visit us at www.ReaderService.com/consumerschoice or write to us at Reader Service Preference Service, P.O. Box 9062, Buffalo, NY 14269. Include your complete name and address.

HARI1B

When Forever, Texas's newest deputy, Gabe Rodriguez, rescues a woman from the scene of an accident, he encounters a mystery, as well.

Here's a sneak peek at A FOREVER CHRISTMAS by USA TODAY bestselling author Marie Ferrarella, available November 2012 from Harlequin® American Romance®.

It was still raining. Not nearly as bad as it had been earlier, but enough to put out what there still was of the fire. Mick was busy hooking up his tow truck to what was left of the woman's charred sedan and Alma was getting back into her Jeep. Neither one of them saw the woman in Gabe's truck suddenly sit up as he started the vehicle.

"No!"

The single word tore from her lips. There was terror in her eyes, and she gave every indication that she was going to jump out of the truck's cab—or at least try to. Surprised, Gabe quickly grabbed her by the arm with his free hand.

"I wouldn't recommend that," he told her.

The fear in her eyes remained. If anything, it grew even greater.

"Who are you?" the blonde cried breathlessly. She appeared completely disoriented.

"Gabriel Rodriguez. I'm the guy who pulled you out of your car and kept you from becoming a piece of charcoal."

Her expression didn't change. It was as if his words weren't even registering. Nonetheless, Gabe paused, giving her a minute as he waited for her response.

But the woman said nothing.

"Okay," he coaxed as he drove toward the town of Forever, "your turn."

The world, both inside the moving vehicle and outside of it, was spinning faster and faster, making it impossible for her to focus on anything. Moreover, she couldn't seem to pull her thoughts together. Couldn't get past the heavy hand of fear that was all but smothering her.

"My turn?" she echoed. What did that mean, her turn? Her turn to do what?

"Yes, your turn," he repeated. "I told you my name. Now you tell me yours."

Her name.

The two words echoed in her brain, encountering only emptiness. Suddenly very weary, she strained hard, searching, waiting for something to come to her.

But nothing did.

The silence stretched out. Finally, just before he repeated his question again, she said in a small voice, hardly above a whisper, "I can't."

Who is this mystery woman?
Find out in A FOREVER CHRISTMAS
by Marie Ferrarella, coming November 2012
from Harlequin® American Romance®.

HAREXP1112

celebrating 15 YEARS

Kathryn Springer

inspires with her tale of a soldier's promise and his chance for love in

The Soldier's Newfound Family

When he returns to Texas from overseas, U.S. Marine Carter Wallace makes good on a promise: to tell a fallen soldier's wife that her husband loved her. But widowed Savannah Blackmore, pregnant and alone, shares a different story with Carter—one that tests everything he believes. Now the marine who never needed anyone suddenly needs Savannah. Will opening his heart be the bravest thing he'll ever do?

←TEXAS TWINS→

Available November 2012

www.LoveInspiredBooks.com

LI87776

Find yourself
BANISHED TO THE HAREM
in a glamorous and tantalizing new tale from

Carol Marinelli

Playboy Sheikh Prince Rakhal Alzirz has time for
one more fling in London before he must return
to his desert kingdom—and Natasha Winters has
caught his eye. He seizes the chance to discover if
Natasha is as fiery in bed as her flaming red hair,
but their recklessness has consequences.... She
might be carrying the Alzirz heir!

BANISHED
TO THE HAREM

Available October 16!